THE BRUEGHEL MOON

First edition, 2014. All rights reserved

Library of Congress Cataloging-in-Publication Data

Cilaze, T'amaz, 1933-
 [Breigelis mt'vare. English]
 The Brueghel moon / Tamaz Chiladze ; translated by Maya Kiasashvili. -- First edition.
    pages cm
    ISBN 978-1-62897-093-7 (p : alk. paper)
    1. Psychotherapists--Fiction. 2. Married people--Fiction.
    3. Psychological fiction. I. Kiasashvili, Maya, translator. II. Title.
 PK9169.C587B713 2015
 899'.9693--dc23

                               2014022139

Partially funded by a grant from the Illinois Arts Council, a state agency

This book is published with the support of the Georgian National Book Centre
and the Ministry of Culture and Monument Protection of Georgia

www.dalkeyarchive.com

Cover design and composition: Mikhail Iliatov
Printed on permanent / durable acid-free paper

TAMAZ CHILADZE

THE BRUEGHEL MOON

A NOVEL

TRANSLATED BY
MAYA KIASASHVILI

DALKEY ARCHIVE PRESS
Champaign / London / Dublin

1

That morning I was coming back from Vake Park from my daily game of tennis. I saw my brother-in-law's jeep at our gate. I was surprised. Badri didn't show up very often. I walked faster.

As I opened the gate, Badri came out of the house with two apparently heavy suitcases. I made way for him, greeted him, to which he just nodded. He didn't say a word.

Ia was sitting at the table in the living room. Tamriko was playing at her feet. I saw several big bags on the floor.

"What's up? Where are we going?" I asked Ia.

"Good. You're back," she said. "I didn't want to leave without you."

"Fine," I sat down, "but are you going without me?" I added with a smile.

"It's not funny," she looked away.

"What's going on?" I knew it wasn't anything pleasant. Of course I guessed that much.

"Remember, I warned you!"

Badri came into the room, so I didn't reply to her. Instead I attempted to joke with Badri:

"What's up, Badri? Where are you taking my wife and daughter?"

"I know nothing," he muttered, took the bags, and went out.

"Remember there was a bird in my coffee cup not long ago?" Ia looked straight into my eyes. Until then she had sat staring at the table. "Apparently, a bird means flying away!"

"So you believe a fortune teller?"

"I do!" She opened her handbag and showed me tickets. "It's better for both of us." She put the tickets back. "It's for the best."

"Yes, but ..." Suddenly it seemed more serious than I had imagined. She wasn't moving in with her parents—she was going somewhere really far away. "When did you decide?" I nearly choked on my saliva.

"A long time ago."

"And waited for the fortune-teller to confirm?"

"Stop!" She raised her hand.

"Stop what?"

"Talking like that," she finished in a whisper.

"Why did you keep it a secret?"

"Emzar called a couple of days ago to say he expected us. I was waiting for his call. I bought the tickets a long time ago. And the documents are ready too. Badri helped me."

"Badri's great, isn't he?"

"My brothers are not for you to make fun of! Shouldn't he have helped?"

"You could've asked *me*."

She looked at me for some time, then averted her gaze and said: "It's for the best."

"Yes, but," I felt anger rising in me, "shouldn't you have asked me what's better? Can you please look at me when I'm talking to you?"

"Don't yell!"

"Turn your head and look at me!"

She swept the air with her hand: "You're going to be alone in this huge apartment. All alone. On your own ... Alone ... Anyway, Badri's taking us to the airport." She was suddenly agitated, clasping her shoulders with her hands as if trying to stop her body from shaking. "Our marriage was a misunderstanding ..."

I interrupted her: "Wait a second, are you serious about going away?"

"I can't believe you haven't noticed it was coming. Where do you think I'm taking all this stuff? I'm not moving in with my parents! I'm fed up with everything here, and there too. Everything around!" She stressed these words. She patted our daughter's head as if to make sure she was there and went on, "You were scared of solitude, but why did you have to drag me into the swamp?"

"The swamp?" I was surprised and offended. "What swamp are you talking about? What kind of scene is this to start today?"

"When you see the outstretched hand of someone screaming for help, don't make a mistake. You can't really help anyone. Instead, you find yourself being dragged into the swamp."

Only then I remembered she had been phoning her brother more often than usual recently. He was in the US, running a seemingly successful business. He called her quite often too, without giving much thought to the time difference. They would talk for a long time. Once I asked who she was talking to for so long. She said to Emzar and that was that. I've got to confess Ia's decision wasn't totally unexpected. For some time I had felt the day was coming. We absolutely had to clarify our relationship because it was getting increasingly impossible to continue with our lives as if nothing was happening. I hoped to resolve it simply, because we weren't the first or the last couple to face the problem. Divorce is as common as meeting someone, even marrying.

She went to the kitchen.

"The kettle must have boiled dry."

I followed her.

"I wanted to have a cup of tea. Boiled dry, as I said."

She held the kettle under the tap.

"I've changed my mind. I don't want it anymore."

"Calm down," I said. "Why are you so agitated? What is it you want?"

"I want to hit you with this kettle!" She laughed. "Want to know why?"

I didn't say anything.

"That's why." She wasn't laughing anymore. "Because of your calmness." She paused, looking for a better word. Then her face lit up. "Damn you and your intelligence!" She rushed out of the kitchen.

We sat at the table again.

"I'd never imagined my profession would come in handy at home," I attempted to joke.

"I hate calm people," she replied.

"Another agitated one is right there, standing outside our house," I didn't intend to say it, but the words just escaped me.

Her expression didn't change: "I can say I was happy for several months."

"Oh, so you know what happiness means, huh? That's interesting." I sounded too calm—even ironic—but not because, as Ia would say, I had no nerves. Quite the opposite. In that extremely tense and stressful situation, I was suddenly gripped by unbearable serenity. Rather strange for me, I should say. "Several months of happiness aren't negligible!"

"It's happiness when you don't think of happiness," Ia replied. Then, cutting herself short, she grabbed the girl. "What have you got in your mouth?" She shook Tamriko by her shoulders. "What is it? Spit it out! Now!" She sprang up, took the crying girl into her arms. "Stop crying! Stop it or I'll throw you out of the window!" she shouted. "Everyone, stop it! Shut up! Damn your kind!"

"Why curse our kind?" I smiled. "You're scaring the child."

She turned to me:

"Are you laughing? What are you laughing at?" She sat down, put Tamriko across her knees, and began to rock her as if she were still a baby. "Sh, sh, sh ... What can I do?" she said quietly as if talking to herself. "One is right here refusing to understand me, the other is waiting outside."

"He is," I said. "Does he know you're leaving?"

"Do you know him?" She tensed visibly, leaned forward, staring at me with bulging eyes.

"Kind of. We even say hello to each other."

"That's exactly why I hate you!" She continued to rock the child. "Sh, sh, sh."

"Is it possible to keep anything a secret in Tbilisi?" I smiled. I could speak calmly now.

"You're smart, very smart and unbearably calm, and if there's anything to bring your end, it's gonna be your smug intelligence and your robotic calmness."

"Destruction by one's brain!"

"Exactly! Don't push me!" she shouted.

"Don't shout," I said quietly. "You're scaring the child."

"She feels and knows everything perfectly well."

"Such as?" I waited for her to answer, but went on when she didn't reply. "What is it she knows? That your lover is waiting in the street so early in the morning?"

"Haven't seen him for three months now," she said quietly.

"You've driven the poor man crazy!"

Suddenly it dawned on me that Ia was running away not so much from me but from her lover. Something unexpected had happened between them because otherwise there were no surprises in our relationship. There was nothing that kept us together and we'd been sleeping in separate rooms for quite some time. Our formal divorce was just a matter of time. Ever since she confessed to seeing someone else, it was bound to happen.

"I'm not sure what the Williams sisters are going to say, but no woman can find fault with you."

"Thanks. Why the Williams sisters?"

"Your Adidas shoes reminded me of them."

"That's an interesting association," I said. "Very witty."

"But you've got a trait that's gonna devastate any woman you happen to come across."

"And that is?"

"You can't love anyone."

I tried to change the topic: "When did you decide to leave?"

"I told you."

"You didn't."

"A long time ago. I wrote to my brother telling him everything."

"Telling him what?"

"That we've got nothing to tell each other. He invited me."

"But why do you need to go that far? Haven't you got another brother nearby? Besides, I can move out so you can stay here."

She put Tamriko down, leaned across the table with her elbows, and asked: "Did you know I was cheating on you? Did you know before I told you?"

She answered her question herself: "You did. You knew all too well, didn't you? Or was it only about the last one?"

It was an extremely painful blow, but I pulled myself together and said: "Please, don't overdo it. Stop making things up!"

"You didn't know about the others because you didn't care, right?"

"Didn't care about what?"

"Whether I was cheating or not. You knew and didn't kill me. Imagine that!"

"How many times should I have killed you?" I came to my senses and even found the strength to confront her. But when she said that wasn't funny, I said, "Incidentally, your most recent lover, waiting now in the street, used to be my tennis partner. Even then!"

"Are you trying to ridicule me? Humiliate me? Why don't you admit I was your patient rather than your wife? We were doctor and patient rather than husband and wife. That's why I need to escape, the sooner the better. I see no other way but to flee."

"You can do it any time, honey."

"I hate that word!"

She said after a short pause: "I hate everything in this house. It was always alien to me and has remained alien. Full of your family."

"My family?"

"The ghosts and phantoms!"

"Oh, I see."

"Tranquil ghosts like you, calm doctors."

"Naturally. My parents were doctors and their parents too. It's a family tradition."

"That's another thing I hate—traditions. How many atrocities are committed in the name of traditions?" She paced around the table, hitting her palm with her fist. "Why don't you ask me to leave the child with you? Why don't you fight? Why don't you hit me?"

"Hit you?" I laughed. "Patients are never beaten in clinics! Shall I tell you what surprises me most?"

She paused: "Something surprises you?"

"You talk, behave, and run away as if it was me who was unfaithful and not you!"

She came closer, looking down at me: "Know what? Since everything's over, let's tell each other the truth. If I don't do it now, I'll be haunted for the rest of my life."

"What more is there to say?"

"I just want you to know it's all your fault."

"What is?"

"Everything!"

"The child looking at you in horror is mine, is she?"

"You're disgusting! A perfect executioner!"

"Why don't you answer?"

"Does it matter?"

"It does!" I yelled at her. "Sit down! Don't stand over me!"

She sat down.

I lowered my voice: "You can leave it unanswered if you wish."

"You know, I'd gladly kill you." She brushed something invisible from her lap, shed a tear. "You've never ever loved me."

"I've never thought about it," I said. "You might be right. I've never loved you."

She sprang up: "I told you so! I told you so!"

"Sit down!"

She sat down.

"Didn't you know?"

"I did!"

"Why does it surprise you then?"

"Surprise me? No, it just breaks my heart to realize how I've lived."

"Tamriko," I stretched my hand to my daughter. "Come to daddy."

The girl moved closer to her mother, staring at me with wide-open eyes, her finger in her mouth.

"What have you told the child about me? Why have you scared her?"

"She doesn't need telling. She knows. Your parents were unhappy too," she said and got to her feet.

"Why were they unhappy?"

She didn't say anything. She flung her bag over her shoulder, picked up Tamriko, and looked around the room: "Am I forgetting anything?"

"If you are, I'll send it to Badri."

"Don't bother. Keep it as a memento. But a memento of what? Of nothing? Does that make sense?"

She made for the door. I followed. She stopped and turned to me:

"I'll leave the signed divorce papers with my lawyer."

"Does it matter?"

"It does. You might wish to marry again."

"I don't think so."

"Good, so you won't make another woman miserable."

"Have you got money?"

"Yes, Badri gave me some. You know my lawyer's phone number. But he'll be calling you anyway. He's going to take care of everything. I never loved you either."

I walked with her to the car. Badri was at the wheel, looking away.

"Can I kiss the child?" I told Ia.

Tamriko clung to her mothers's bosom, averting her face. I kissed her on the shoulder. My mouth was full of the fluff from her coat. They got into the car. Ia wound down the window and said: "Blame yourself for everything. Farewell ..."

2

And she was gone. Lost like a stone thrown into the water. I spent the next three months in a limbo-like state. To be honest, I never thought the whole thing would affect me to such an extent. Not only affect but actually hurl me out of my normal life. Not immediately, but gradually everything seemed to have lost meaning, faded out. I went to work, answered phone calls, but it was pretty mechanical. Judging from my actions and speech it might have been hard to detect the changes which I clearly felt. Apparently no one noticed, otherwise they would have told me, indicated in some way. Of course all my friends and family as well as my co-workers knew about my family drama. People are interested in such things. But they refrained from discussing it with me, which is understandable. However, I felt everyone wanted to hear the story first-hand, to find out what happened in a seemingly quiet, typical Tbilisi family.

I could see something was very wrong with me. It looked like the onset of a nervous breakdown, but I couldn't stop it. And still, most upsetting were the dreams, visions, or images — either caused by my depressed mood or the other way round — intensified my dejected state with the strange sequence of a serial. When alone, whether asleep or awake, I saw the world differently, heard different voices. The most painful was occasionally picturing myself as a helpless old man. I wanted to confess to someone how one feels when abandoned, left alone with oneself, how bitter and dejected — I didn't want to use the word, but here it is — a madman can be. I wished to share it as a secret that might have been heard out with pleasure, while I would shake it off and feel free not so much from solitude, which is virtually impossible, but from the visions triggered by solitude, which forced me to dwell in another, non-real world.

I thought if I opened the door, an alien, vicious element would dash in like that masked soldier who filled our TV screens. And he would demand the most precious thing I had. I'd gladly give it, but the problem is I don't know what I hold most dear and, generally speaking, what is most precious for people? Does anyone know?

Throughout those three months, in my dreams and my wakefulness, a tapping on the door constantly accompanied my state of deep depression.

So, here I am, a hundred years old, sitting in an armchair, and I'm aware it's not real, but I'm thinking aloud. The discovery troubled me because I also felt, or rather guessed, that life doesn't go on — it ends, disappears, fades out in such a way that it's hard to say whether it's life at all. But if it's not life, then what is? My favorite Georgian poetic word for life literally means "a minute in this world." A strange notion, sounds like the spirit escaping the body.

My armchair is near the radiator in a big, empty room. Sounds reach me from the outside, but I'm not at all certain whether it's a street, a forest, or a vast field. I believe it's someone singing. Half-raised in my armchair, supporting my weight with my hands on the armrests, I repeat, tensely but for some reason joyfully: "Can you hear someone singing? Someone's singing!" I don't know whom I address, to whom I repeat the words ...

On the walls of my empty heart there are addresses and phone numbers just like those written on phone booth walls. But unlike those, mine aren't that many and I remember them all. I know exactly whose addresses and numbers they are. How distant and detached everything seems now from what they remind me. Mostly shadowy recollections of brief, accidental encounters. Clothes strewn on the floor, an empty bottle of sparkling wine of course, which I intensely hate, lying on its side. A meaningless, closed-eye whisper, the same word repeated a hundred, a thousand times. Then lying back in the dark, completely still, fulfilled and spent, dozing off for a couple of seconds and then, surely, groping for a cigarette and a lighter ...

Little by little I was becoming convinced I lived a fuller life in my dreams than in reality, especially because my dreams resembled the reality. Some of the dreams were recurrent. It was thanks to my dreams that I lived in a constant state of expectation which had no name and filled me with strange melancholy. Who or what was I waiting for, who was destined to appear in my life to change it?

It was Ia's departure that persistently, and with amazing clarity, featured in my dreams. I couldn't get rid of it, just like Tamriko's coat fluff. I wanted to die and to see her, but not to remember her! But how was I to free myself from her? Isn't it our dreams that testify to our vulnerability when facing ourselves? The scene, recurrent without any alteration, like the video evidence presented in the courtroom, gradually convinced me I was guilty, but I didn't know what crime I had committed, what I had to blame myself for. I could easily admit to having committed a crime in court, but I wouldn't be able to say which one exactly, if asked. Anyway, I took the blame with all its consequences, without even attempting to justify myself. And once I took the burden, I had to carry it— not merely as a heavy load but more like a natural defect, such as a hump. I had to swallow my pride and tolerate the humiliation I would otherwise never imagine I was capable of bearing. Don't others do the same? I was asking myself. Don't they tolerate things, all sorts of atrocities, which they eventually get used to, to the extent that they seem to be necessities of life? Broadly speaking, isn't human life the endurance of things absolutely unimaginable in one's young days? Life is tolerance of atrocity! Oh God, how easily the adolescent blind faith crumbles!

I suddenly felt with all my senses that I hastened as if I was late for something, as if I was expected somewhere else. And I believed in the unbelievable: that beyond this world, beyond this reality, just several steps away there is another reality but, like a train in a small station, it's about to leave and I've got to catch it at all costs because I need to get into that other reality which, for some obscure reason, looks like a doctor's surgery with a couch covered with a white oilcloth behind a partition. My imagination didn't stretch further, and all I wanted was to stretch on that couch so that all my visions and haunting images would disappear, vanish, disperse in the dark, so that I could forget them once and for all. And all the while, I was—the most important bit—not a doctor but a patient, which made me immensely happy! I'm sick, I thought. Really sick. I might be going mad. How can I cure others if I need to be cured myself? I shared my concern with one of my colleagues I was on friendly terms with. I believe in this case the term asks for an explanation because our friendship was limited to phone conversations or going across from the clinic to a diner and having a drink or two with our meal. Once he read me a poem of his. Dreadful. I did say, however, that it was fine. He said he knew. What do I do with these dreams I have, the nightmares, the depression, the apathy? I don't want anything, nothing interests me anymore. I don't read newspapers. But I still go to the clinic, do my job. In short, I said, I lie to the patients and myself.

"Are you by any chance drinking without me?" he asked with an impish squint. "Spill it."

"I'm not," I said.

"Too bad."

That night he called me to say I'd get used to it because he, for instance, had had three wives. It meant I had wasted my breath talking about my worries and anxieties. No one understands another person. No one, not even the closest one, not any more than anyone else. They might take your pain into their hearts but they will never really know how it aches. Suppose they internalize your pain in full. They can't help you anyway. Who is going to pump out of you all the melancholy and worry hanging down like heavy smoke?

One midnight I opened my eyes and yelled for Mother. I craved her, I wanted to hide my face in her lap, wanted her to pat my head with her trembling hand. I wished to weep earnestly, smearing my face with bitter tears like a child. I sprang up, dashed down the hall to my parents' bedroom and did not open so much as fling the door wide. "Mother! Mother!" I shouted. I sat down, then and there. My heart thumped so hard, as if it willed itself to jump out of my chest. Took me a few moments to get my breath back ... One of my acquaintances told me the following day I had to light a candle. So

I went to the little new church in Vake and lit a candle for Virgin Mary: Mother Mary, can you please tell Mother I feel lonely? I miss her. I've always feared solitude, more often than not turning a blind eye to lots of things for fear of solitude. It was all my doing. I deserved all that befell me. Was it true I made the woman miserable? The one I loved! I had a huge problem saying the word as it felt like scratching my throat from the inside. My entire alarmed essence seemed to hint I couldn't go on alone or rather, I needed someone to talk to or someone who'd listen with their heart or say things coming from their heart.

That night I dreamt I followed someone in a top hat along the snowy streets. He looked as if he'd stepped out of a 19th century painting. He was dressed exactly like Mephistopheles from one of the Tbilisi theatre productions, where everything seems all right but something is amiss. Something was a little off about his appearance, but no one, not even Mephistopheles—if he were dead and then came back—could have put his finger on what was wrong with his clothes. I thought, God, he's so familiar, I definitely know him. Suddenly it dawned on me it was Lado Tavzarashvili, the academic! Where to, Lado? Is it the airport again? He didn't reply but I persisted: Don't even think about it. Once gone, no one has ever returned, and you should know better. Then the man I thought resembled Lado Tavzarashvili and I roamed the empty city streets, finally coming to the river. I seemed to be looking at a frozen river for the first time. It was lifeless and faceless, like a big stiff fish taken out of the freezer. Indeed, there was the river like a frozen fish wedged between the concrete banks, too big for its frozen, frayed fins. No, it was in my dream I thought I was looking at a frozen river for the first time. In reality I'd seen one the night Tamriko was born. I got a call in the middle of the night and rushed to the maternity hospital. My father-in-law and brother-in-law were already there. On the way back, my father-in-law refused to be driven home, telling Badri he wanted to take a walk with me. The weather was not inviting for a stroll. We walked without a word. Till dawn. He stopped at the embankment, drew a pack of cigarettes from his pocket. He offered me one. We had a hard time lighting them. There was a bitter, icy wind blowing.

"Where've you been, Levan?" he asked. "Asleep?"

I said I was. I wanted to say I came as soon as I got the call but he didn't let me.

"We nearly lost Ia. She had to have a caesarian."

"I know. The doctor told me," I said.

"The doctor can't have told you what I'm going to say now: I'll kill you with my own hands!"

"Excuse me?" I didn't catch the first bit.

"Kill you with my own hands," he repeated, sending the cigarette butt into the river with a flick. "The motherfucker's frozen!" He walked away.

I didn't follow. I stayed behind for some time staring at the frozen river. Of course I knew exactly what he meant. It wasn't the first time he said it. In fact he'd said it over and over again: if I ever did anything, even the smallest thing ("as small as my little fingernail" in his words) to upset his precious daughter, who had refused to marry an American millionaire, her brother's business partner fully approved by her dad, but chose to cling to a loony doctor—his words again—he'd kill me. Actually, he was quite capable of doing it. I stood there, on the embankment, thinking how a man's uncontrolled fury and unrestrained vanity could easily bring him to sheer idiocy. Was it my fault she had to have a caesarian to save the baby?

However, the dream man wasn't my father-in-law, neither was it Lado Tavzarashvili. Just resembled both. We were strangers to each other, quite different, like the inhabitants of different worlds or even galaxies.

"Can't you see the dog?" the man asked me. "We've come to the frozen river specifically for it."

And by some magic I immediately spotted a poor dog, with its tail between its hind legs, miserably crouching on the bank. If not for its dark bright eyes, I would've taken it for a snow heap.

"It's going to be your travelling companion," he laughed.

I was gripped with fear, trembling all over.

"Am I going blind?" I finally managed to get the words out.

"Quite the contrary," he said and added after a short pause, "You've just had your eyes properly opened."

"To see what?" I asked or rather clutched at the question as if it were the proverbial straw that would save or, more likely, break me.

"Eventually you're going to realize that one can learn only from oneself. We learn in order to forget and forget in order to learn more." The man walked up and down in front of me, in long, steady, noisy strides, as if measuring the distance for a duel or a penalty kick. "However, we don't know why we learn or forget what we've already learned, but it's precisely this non-knowledge that allows us to keep balance on a piece of slippery ice. Indeed, we are stuck between forgetting and learning, just like between two trains moving in the opposite directions. You don't even know who I am, who you're talking to."

"I know!" I cried with joy as if it was my chance to say the most essential thing which would put everything in its right place. I wanted to say something I failed to tell my father-in-law or Lado Tavzarashvili. The man's words were so familiar, I took them for what either of them could have said.

"No," the man warned me, patting my shoulder lightly. "You don't, and what's more, you can't know. You see me as an old opera singer ..."

"Oh, no, no," I waved my arms. I was terribly embarrassed because that was exactly what I thought.

He went on: "An operatic Mephistopheles! Right? Don't say anything! Don't interrupt me! You believe I'm an actor entertaining by talking to himself at the frozen river bank."

"Talking to himself?" I meant to play for time with these words which didn't make much sense because suddenly I realized it was all in my dream so I had to stay as calm as possible. But more than anything it proved most difficult to keep a level head. My voice quivered, the sounds came hoarse and when I repeated the question, I hardly recognized my own voice. It was completely alien, even more, it sounded suspiciously like that of this tall, theatrical man.

We seemed to be talking to each other in the same voice. We had a common voice which we tossed at each other as if it were a tennis ball.

"Yes," he replied promptly, "to himself. As in, in less than thirty years, which will literally fly by because nothing is faster in this world than time, you can turn into someone like me, exactly as I am now, and not only in appearance. And that's not the worst, but you seem to find it highly amusing ..."

"No, I don't!" I interrupted.

"Let me finish," he sounded angry. "Similar in fate too! And destiny isn't something you can change like clothes. Fate isn't a theatrical prop. Neither is it a goatee you can shave off. You were reminded of an operatic Mephistopheles, weren't you? In thirty years you'll be out in the frost, standing by the frozen river, exactly like me, because you won't have anywhere to go. And though you hate snow— or rather there's nothing else you detest as much as snow—you'll come to this frozen river, which is comparable to your entire life. You'll be welcoming the New Year in the company of a dog."

"In thirty years?" I asked with a trembling voice because the tennis ball tossed at me had lost its hardness. "So what?" I said, "lots of people lead a lonely life."

"So you are ready to accept it?" the man asked in surprise and pursed his lips. "Don't you fear solitude?"

"No," I answered, thinking: Oh God, how come he knows I dread solitude most of all? "No!" I repeated trying to sound more convincing and the tennis ball returned some of its bounciness. "I'm not scared. The world is full of lonely people."

The man laughed and walked away. He looked back a couple of times until he disappeared in the distance. I could hear his laughter for a long time though.

I woke up. My mouth was dry, with a disgusting taste. I got up. Drank some water. I felt as if I had betrayed someone or something. In the bathroom mirror I told myself not to worry as it wasn't me I had betrayed. But as I said this I knew I was lying because my heart felt strangely empty, a familiar feeling from my childhood when

I used to lie pretty often. I was lying and a sense of vague guilt stabbed my heart.

"You know," I told myself in the mirror, "I'm going to live in the company of a dog! I'm getting old …"

I went back to the bedroom and got into the bed. I took a book. Couldn't read it. Lay there till morning with wide-open eyes.

The early onset of old age that I experienced while talking to my reflection in the bathroom wasn't that unexpected despite my age. Apparently, I grew old prior to the painful realization. I used to calmly cope with everything—the home, the clinic, everything and everyone. I seemed to have been destined to treat people and things with limitless patience, so I didn't resist. Actually, instead of resistance, I took refuge in the fact—just like a homeless man, though I knew, and that was particularly painful—that it wasn't a house but a snail shell …

They say, and probably for good reason, that real life occurs in dreams. We make sense in our dreams, see and hear ourselves in our dreams, realizing and remembering things we seem to have forgotten in our conscious life. In short, it is in our dreams that we know for sure who we truly are …

This went on for quite some time. I lived in my dream performances, participating in them against my free will, not knowing my lines. Probably I had nothing to say because I was meant to be an extra or was waiting for the grand finale or rather the invisible director had designated me for it. That's what happened in the end, but it's too early for that …

The commonplace phrases so essential in our everyday life that I uttered almost mechanically in the clinic, supermarket, and subway didn't belong to the grand performance. They were so insignificant, I didn't count them as words at all. In short, my life demanded so much energy and caused so much anxiety that I would drag myself to bed, completely exhausted. Even that didn't bring relief: my bed turned into a torture machine. "Did I love her so much?" I thought. "Should I have killed her?" My head was full of these horrid thoughts. My heart would go tender, I would choke on the lump in my throat. And then I would spring up. Roam the empty house.

"What you say," my colleague told me, "sounds like an alcoholic's hallucinations."

I believe it was the other way round, because every time I got drunk, I slept peacefully, without any dreams.

It was the first time I drank at home. I didn't even think of taking a glass, just drank straight from the bottle. I didn't bother to do it properly, in a civilized way like people do, or rather in a conventionally civilized way as no one can say with certainty what human is and what is not. I got drunk very quickly. In general, I can handle my alcohol, a designated toastmaster at friends' parties. When I woke up the next morning, I felt like I was surfacing from pitch darkness. In truth, I preferred my nightmares to such dark. As though a dead man had a choice and opted for death, that's how I felt. Then, as I was rummaging among Ia's medicine cabinet, I found Lexotanil pills—so she left something behind! As I swallowed the pink pill, it suddenly struck me that I had been invited to one of the world-renowned clinics in Switzerland thanks to my father-in-law! He might have been paying my high salary from his pocket. And all the while I had been sure, and extremely proud, that I was chosen from numerous Georgian doctors solely owing to my published works. This tranquilizer seemed to be an eye-opener too. Apparently, he decided to get his daughter out of the country, just like his elder son. Ia worked alongside me in the same clinic. And that's when I had to guess my articles might have been completely unknown and unread in Switzerland. Apart from my salary, my flat and car could have been his gifts.

Ia and I had spent ten years in Switzerland. And it was in bits and pieces that news from Georgia usually reached us. There wasn't much on the country in the press either. For the spoiled Swiss society, it must have been unconceivable even to imagine how another nation suffered so much at the end of the twentieth century. How could no other country support them when their territories were snatched, their gas supply cut, all of which looked like clear attempts to physically annihilate the nation? No. They didn't understand it, neither did they sympathize because they had safeguarded themselves from any possible problems a long time ago. Ia and I seemed to be the prisoners of our own security there, but we never discussed it. I worked hard and studied as well — the clinic was a true university for psychiatrists like myself. Luckily, I could already speak several languages, thanks to my parents. In our free time we walked a lot and travelled by car, so we saw a good part of the country. We used to play tennis nearly every day. Ia was certainly better at it. Used to mock me, calling me 'old'. In those days old age seemed so far away that I even didn't contemplate it at all. We used to invite our colleagues from other countries to our house parties for Tamar's Day (our mothers were named after the saint), May 26, our National Day, and Ia's birthday. Babies were taboo in our family. Ia wouldn't hear of them as she had a pathological fear of childbirth. Our relationship, our marital bed, was like a battlefield. She used to tell me I had to choose between her and a baby.

Usually, I went blank. I didn't know how to react.

"Want me to die?" she used to ask very calmly, and that's why it sounded so cynical to me at those moments.

She took some pills. And made me take traditional precautions from day one. My father-in-law had organized a grand wedding party. For several hours I stoically withstood the idiotic toasts from the loud toastmaster. However, they couldn't make me dance, even though five hundred guests cheered standing up: "Let the groom dance!" Ia also asked me, but quietly, as if whispering softly to the plate: "Please, Levan, Dad will be hurt." Then, when finally we were left alone in our room, she undressed without a word and got into the bed. But first, she said she was sorry she wouldn't be able to wear that dress anymore. She lay there, uncovered, looking at me with a smile as I hastily undressed.

"What's the hurry?" she said.

I sat down beside her.

"Swear," she demanded.

"To what?"

"That you're going to love me forever."

"Good time for an oath! We've just said our vows!"

She turned her head and said softly: "I'm scared."

"Of what?" I bent to kiss her. She returned it and repeated: "I'm scared."

"Of what?"

"A baby."

That's when I should have gone, fled, left everything behind, moved to a distant country where no one could reach me. But at the time, there was no force to tear me away from the electrifyingly alluring body, from the sweetly enthralling lips. I would've agreed to anything. Anything at all.

"Don't forget the condom," she said in a matter of fact way. I had never heard the word from her before.

"Where do I get one in the middle of the night?"

"It's right there, on the bedside table. Within your reach."

Of course we had a baby, but later, when we had returned from Switzerland, some four years ago. And for sure, our house needed renovating badly. Ia stayed with her parents for nearly a month, while I, probably the most impractical man in the world, had to deal with the workmen. I'm pretty certain, at least that's what I deduced after a month spent overseeing the workmen, that if a man can renovate his house, he can easily run a country. Apparently, Tamar, Ia's mother—an extremely caring and sympathetic lady, who seemed to be apologizing to everyone for everything as if it were all her fault—had worked at trying to make her change her mind. And, waking up one morning in our newly-renovated bedroom, Ia squinted from under the blanket: "Are we going to have a baby?"

"That'd be wonderful," I said. "I wish we had one!"

"Don't touch me," she said. "Ever."

Some time later my father-in-law visited us, which he hadn't done before. He was sitting in an armchair, with Ia on his knees. She had her arms around him with her head on his chest. When I opened the door, they took no notice of me. I stood in the doorway. The complete silence was broken by the rhythmic ticking of the wall clock. I felt unwanted. As if I wasn't welcome. I went out of the room, noiselessly closing the door. I went into my study. Sat at my desk. Took a literary magazine. Opened it. I sat staring at the pages for what seemed quite a long time. Then my father-in-law came in. I rose to my feet. He told me to stay seated.

"Please have a seat," I drew up a chair for him.

He didn't take it.

"You know," he said, "you're going to have a baby."

"Excuse me?" I couldn't believe my ears.

He turned and left without another word.

"Aren't you happy?" Ia asked me when we were alone.

"Shouldn't you have told me?" I was sulking because she didn't tell me first.

"Tell me if you're happy."

"And you?" I asked in return.

"Me?" She paused, as if debating whether to say it or not. "Me?" she repeated. "Yeah, I've decided to have it."

"Great," I said.

"Nothing else?" Ia looked at me in surprise.

"What else can I say?"

"Right. What else can you say? I know everything. I'm going to be 34 soon ..."

"I know," I said. "I know your age!"

"Are you angry?"

"No, why should I be? But aren't you scared anymore?"

"In fact, I am," she replied. "I still am, very much."

"So, it seems," I said, "our fears have come true."

"Yes, something I dreaded. I've ruined your life ... I'm scared, very scared. I don't know what's wrong with me."

"Nothing," I replied. "You've just turned into a woman. A normal woman. True, slightly later than others, but they say, better late than ..."

"Nobody knows it," she interrupted, "which is better—late or never." She paused, thinking, then went on as if asking someone else, not me, "A woman?" She looked at me. "You might be right, you know."

The baby was born. Then my father-in-law died, unexpectedly, last year. He was invited to the Prosecutor's Office, along with many well-known figures. He was kept there for two days. He was said to have paid a lot of money. Then he went on living as usual, but never went anywhere without his wife. She accompanied him all the time, in his car. They used to drive to their summer house in Saguramo, and stay there for a couple of days. He took to gardening, pottering around busily all day long. It was there, in Saguramo, that they sat watching TV, and when his wife asked him something, he didn't reply ...

The fact that I recalled everything clearly and meticulously could have been the fault of an early onset of old age which, as I already said, I had felt while talking to myself in the mirror. The whole thing sounded not like my own experience, but as if someone else had recounted it to me. That explains why most of the things have remained vague, incomprehensible and bizarre till today. It wasn't just my life, because I believe most people's lives are stained, but unlike them, I decided to try to find sense in mine when I wasn't able to think straight because of my depressed state. That's why I failed to guess from the beginning that some things are better left alone, untouched, in the dark. Not just some things, but everything if, of course, one wishes to live in peace. And not particularly peacefully but ordinarily, just like the rest, following their example. Actually, peace is an extremely relative concept. It's not obligatory for everyone to understand it in the same way, which is utterly unrealistic anyway. But isn't everything relative and conventional? "People are similar in being so different," as my favourite English poet says.

"Buddy," my colleague told me, "you think too much of the woman."

We were having dumplings and beer in a diner.

"You can't go on like this. You've got to move on."

"It's not that easy, I've discovered," I said. "I got used to her. Ten years together, just like two castaways shipwrecked on an island, alone. I've got lots of good memories of her." I wasn't obliged to say anything to him, but it was the drink that made me talk, as if I wished to open up and get it out of my heart.

"The other day," my colleague said, "I read about a tribe in Africa. These people eat their own excrement. And some women, apparently, keep theirs for their loved ones, as a special treat."

"Why are you telling me this?" I asked.

"No reason." He drank his beer. "A woman's a woman, everywhere."

Life seemed to get back to normal little by little. It's true when they say time cures all, but as Sancho Panza said, what can be worse than something that can be cured only by time? Somehow I kept remembering the night before Ia left for the US, thinking that night could have been decisive, impelling things to take a different course. For the whole year Ia and I had slept separately. She was with Tamriko in the master bedroom, while I slept on the couch in my study. That night when Ia came in, I was already in bed but awake. She had white silk pajamas on. She told me to make room for her and lay down beside me. For quite a long time we didn't speak. Then she asked for a cigarette. I took two from the package. One for her. We lit them. We smoked in silence, then she said, "No one knows what's a lie and what's the truth." Then she got up and left . . .

Gradually I regained my usual good disposition. I resumed my regular walks in Vake Park. My old partners greeted me there. And one day I did something quite strange, something I still find baffling—I went to my father-in-law's grave! As a rule I don't often go to the cemetery, only occasionally visiting my parents' grave in the Pantheon. I pay a woman to take good care of the place.

The granite bench by the grave was very dusty. I spread my handkerchief and sat down. I already knew it was stupid of me. Why was I there? Was it normal for me? However, sometimes normal people do such crazy things that they would stun even the craziest people. My being at his grave was sheer madness, for want of a better word. But that's exactly what set me thinking. It seemed I had something to say to him, something which made me lose peace of mind, something which I would never dare tell him while he was alive. I always found it hard to talk to rude, gruff, unforthcoming people. I found it hard because rudeness or impoliteness angered me to the extent that I couldn't talk to them in the manner they deserved. In other words, I couldn't be rude to them in return. Besides, anger made me forget the main thing I needed to say, reflecting on it much later when in bed, I'd start thinking I had to say it in this or that way, but it was hopelessly too late anyway ...

The man now gloomily staring at me from the picture framed by the granite slab had spoiled his daughter, my wife, from early childhood to the extent that she grew into an ambitious, haughty, nervous egotist, demanding constant attention, praise, reassurance, love, and care, special treatment like a rare exotic flower. Once, in Switzerland, she told me she had spent an entire year in bed as a child. Not knowing what was wrong with her, she said, her parents tried to fulfill her every wish and whim. It was strange timing because we were sitting on the sofa watching TV and I watched her profile thinking my god, she hasn't got a single friend, not a single woman she can call a friend. Telepathy exists, of course it does. Everything exists that you believe doesn't. "Nothing is but what is not," Shakespeare said. I could have yelled it down my father-in-law's grave, blamed him for our divorce. There was a grain of truth in that, but a very small one. Instead I said, "Please forgive me. It seems I've never loved your daughter. I destroyed her. I deserve to be killed. I'm sorry you didn't kill me when the time was right." I didn't mean it ironically. I was dead serious. I really believed so or rather someone talking instead of me thought and believed so, being more outspoken, brave, and bitter, while I just listened. Unimaginable, but I wanted to prompt that someone else to tell my father-in-law that sometimes we commit the gravest of crimes in the name of love.

I left the cemetery, seemingly relieved of the burden. Apparently I had needed to go to his grave, because it had haunted me for so long. Could that have been one of the reasons for my unusual anxiety? I said I never loved her. Isn't imaginary and then believed love disgusting, sheer evil? But I was sure I loved her. I had never thought about it, never doubted it for a second. Probably because I preferred it that way. Preferred to love her. I might have forgotten, but does anyone ever remember that an imaginary, forced love can be ruthless? It never forgives you. Someday, somewhere, unexpectedly, it's bound to hit you on the head. Never mind yourself because you pay for your spiritual laziness, but doesn't someone else fall victim to the misunderstanding?

That night I dreamed he stretched his arm from the grave—I recognized his gold Rolex—and grabbed the handkerchief I had left on the bench, crumpled it in his fist, and dragged it down under ...

That was my last nightmare!

After that things went on as usual. Ia didn't phone from the States even once, neither did I try to find her number. I played tennis and went to the clinic as usual. Not very often, but occasionally my colleague and I would go over the road to our regular diner. That was it. Several months passed in uneventful monotony. I shied away from meeting new people. In the evenings I would stay home reading, or diligently, stubbornly, and meticulously putting everything I did or thought about into my diary. In general, it may be interesting to read about a 53-year-old man whose wife cheated on him and ran away, especially if it's told in detailed, naïve candor. I had started to keep a diary in Switzerland. With pedantic precision, I used to write down everything I thought interesting. In fact, everything was new and interesting. In my diary, I even came across jokes popular among my colleagues at the time. Now I couldn't remember why I liked them or why I found them funny. Jokes become dated faster than movies. I also seemed to have read a lot, mainly medical literature. I had taken notes on Freud and his followers' works, which of course were out of my reach in Georgia. I had read Frisch and Dürrenmatt, but apparently wasn't particularly impressed. I went to a symphony in Geneva. The German Requiem by Brahms! The whole page was full of exclamation marks. I remember leaving the hall utterly dazzled. I put the diary aside, found the disc and was listening to the record not only that evening but the whole week.

Time passed. Nothing interesting was happening in my life. But an old suspicion, dating back to my student days, reasserted itself, possibly because, frankly speaking, I couldn't help myself, let alone others: I remembered coming across a phrase of Aristotle's which nearly made me change my mind about my chosen career. But the profession, apart from being extremely interesting, was hereditary. I was simply obliged to carry on the family tradition. One of our family friends used to joke that doctors were like monarchs in that "the crown" is passed down hereditarily, but unlike royal dynasties, the results are often better among doctors. As I said, when I read Aristotle's phrase, I was bewildered. The philosopher said: "When dealing with the human soul, there is nothing that can serve as entirely trustworthy, solid evidence." At the time I thought fortune-teller was a better word for me than doctor, or even prison warden caring for a poor soul confined in a lifelong cell, guarding the happy society. I shared my not-so-happy thoughts with my dad. I did fear he might have taken them as a sign of my stupidity, but who'd give me better answers than him? For some reason dad found it amusing. He was putting on his coat in the hall. He took time buttoning up, opened the front door and said before stepping out: "When I was your age, I thought exactly like you, that treating the unknown was like fortune-telling, nothing else." Yes, but, I ran after him without a coat or hat. What about Hippocrates's oath? Is it nothing else but loyalty to helplessness? Belief in something non-existent? An ode to fanaticism? He laughed loudly and said: "I believe because it's absurd! Now go home before you catch cold." That was the suspicion gnawing at me: to hell with me, never mind that I deceive myself, but what about the patients I wreck instead of curing? In truth, lies helped both sides, me and my patients, soothing us alike because we lost the sense of alarm, but gained alluringly merciless hope. Dad used to say, "Curious, my dear gentleman, curious!"

After that things took a fantastic turn. Of course I'm using the word for want of a better one, but the events I witnessed and was part of were more characteristic of science fiction or fantasy, those extremely popular genres. I think we've defined the term too hastily and rather superficially. Is everything we call fiction the result of fantasy? It's inconceivable that a human mind can construct or construe anything which isn't prompted by some secret, yet unknown reality. Even the most daring dreams have been triggered by reality. No human can dream of things which don't exist, which are unattainable or ephemeral. The main problem is that the reality still remains impenetrable and inexplicable while it truly is the magic workshop of our dreams. In addition, humans don't know the place they live in, their own planet. Just like survivors of a shipwreck fortunate enough to reach an uninhabited island, geological, biological, and archaeological expeditions still roam the continents. A human being wasn't born on Earth. We arrived. Despite plenty of interesting discoveries (or maybe thanks to them) one thing is clear—our planet is absolutely alien to us, in other words it's part of the reality we are trying to comprehend so painstakingly but to no avail. And that's good because if we succeeded, if we fully understood our existence, it would certainly lose that life-giving grain thanks to which we are called humans and not animals. Secrets are for a human mind only, a secret needs a sensible creature, because only common sense can push you towards solving a mystery. Or give you the strength to live.

I'm turning the pages of my diary and, becaue I've wished to re-read it, that means the joy of life has returned to me. Rereading one's own diary equals remembering oneself. And that's exactly what we lose from time to time or forget, caught in the turmoil of our everyday life. And another page: one might even believe the majority of the planet's population was the result of space migration. Nearly the same happened when Columbus discovered America. Hordes of settlers from practically all corners of the world moved to the new land.

Our planet was discovered by an alien Columbus and immediately colonies from various planets moved towards the Earth at different times and in different numbers. Doesn't the variety of how we look prove this? How can people living on the different continents of our tiny planet look so strikingly different? Apparently, creatures from outer space had been settling on Earth. A human being—an anatomically perfect, thinking mechanism—has evolved over time as a long-term experiment of nature and this has shaped us into what we are. But how can God's power and will have been limited to a tiny planet? A human is a human, even in space! And the Georgians seem to have been well aware of that fact. Amiran, our mythological hero, did bring a bride from the sky, but Qamar was an ordinary woman, so ordinary in fact, that she taught him how to kill his father. The first thing the outer space settlers introduced to Earth was a wheel—the symbol of the sun, intuitively familiar and so precious for all dwellers of the universe. The symbol is deeply engraved in the collective memory of mankind, firmly linked to the idea of continuous movement. The fact that the Incas and Aztecs had never heard of a wheel until the Americas were discovered only proves that they, though the creators of a highly-developed civilization, were the indigenous people of the planet Earth ...

All of this was written at various times. The notes have different dates but having written them meant I had more or less recovered from my illness. In a way, my layman's notes serve as a kind of evidence ...

It all started with a visit from my former patient. The term "former", though, is least applicable to my patients because I was so used to their regular visits.

She was a tall woman, wearing a dress too short for her age. She sat down. Crossed her legs, as if demonstrating how slender and long they were. She took a package of cigarettes and a box of matches from her handbag and put them on the floor. Her bag was of a discolored canvas, more like a soldier's rucksack than an elegant handbag. She lit a cigarette. I pushed an ashtray toward her. We were sitting at the table.

"I'm going to take your time," she said. "If you aren't ready for it, please let me know and I'll leave immediately."

"I've got plenty of time," I said. "I'm all ears." I indicated she could start talking.

"I'd like to tell you something, doctor. Don't you smoke? Ah, of course you do! It's you who got me used to it."

"Did I?" I asked with a smile.

She didn't reply, just went on: "You've already heard the story I'm about to tell you, but you don't remember it, do you? Apparently, you don't recognize me either. Yes, I've changed a lot. Twenty-seven years have gone by and I'm a completely different person now."

She waved the smoke away, following it with her eyes. Strangely, she smiled at me and said:

"You were the doctor of my ward."

She rolled the sleeve of her left arm and showed me her wrist. There was a very faint, thin scar with hardly visible ragged edges, as if covered by thin paper.

"Do you remember?"

"I'm sorry, I don't ..."

And then suddenly I did: "Can it be you?"

I sprang to my feet.

"My god!"

I sat down again.

"Are you Nunu?"

"Twenty-seven years have passed since then," she said, "maybe more. I'm not sure."

All at once he remembered it all as if his eyes began to see what he hadn't noticed before. Dark, dungeon-like wards full of rats and cockroaches, dirty windows with metal bars, long musty corridors reeking of food, walls covered in mildew because of the seeping water, multi-colored stinking pools in the toilets. "For a man who goes insane to be punished so inhumanely is pure injustice," a patient told him. Against the backdrop of this latrine-like building from hell, a woman was sitting on the edge of a neatly made bed, combing her hair, looking at herself in a pocket mirror—an angel accidentally fallen from the heavens. The woman was diagnosed with an anxiety syndrome caused by a psychological trauma and distinct abulia with a complete loss of volition.

"Do you also think I'm mad?" she asked him during one of the medical checks.

At the time he avoided a direct answer:

"Everything will be clear with time," he said, or rather muttered, and his own words affected him to the extent that for many nights he would wake up with a jolt, choking on a thorny ball wedged in his throat.

The story she told would convince anyone she was insane. She had a room to herself from the beginning, thanks to "influential acquaintances" as they said, but that wasn't true as good connections were used to get people out of there, not for keeping them in, even in relative comfort. At first the woman didn't talk at all, which was taken as a clear symptom of mutism. But then she suddenly started to talk and talked without stopping. Whoever it was—a doctor, nurse, janitor, or another patient—she would be telling the same story over and over again. Some listened, others didn't, clearly avoiding her. Every patient had a sad story of their own. No one visited her. Her manners and speech were typical of a middle-class intellectual. Once, she asked Levan for a cigarette.

"But you don't smoke, do you?" the young doctor was surprised.

"I don't. I've never smoked but I want it very much."

At the time Levan had been working for about two years in the clinic named after his eminent father. He handed her the pack.

She took a cigarette: "You can light it I guess."

She inhaled greedily.

"Careful!" Levan cried.

Unperturbed, she let the smoke through her nostrils and said: "It's great!"

"Is it really your first cigarette?" Levan asked.

"It is."

She was taken somewhere a couple of times, for a long while at that. Levan used to regularly supply her with cigarettes. One day a commission from the Ministry of Health visited the clinic. Levan watched through the window how the academic Tavzarashvili walked into the garden, hopped across the decorative tiles as if a child playing hopscotch, then halted at the bust of Iase, Levan's father, took off his straw hat, drew a handkerchief from his pocket and wiped his bald head. One couldn't say for sure whether he was showing respect to the deceased colleague or just wiping the sweat.

For starters, Tavzarashvili accepted a petition from one of his retinue signed by the clinic patients. The patients demanded that Nunu "be evicted" from the clinic as she was occupying a much needed place for a real patient. The petition was endorsed by the Minister with a hieroglyphic signature. Tavzarashvili put the paper on the table, spread it out with his hand and studied it carefully. Then he banged the table with his fist and got to his feet, saying there was no need to take anyone's time. He wiped his sweaty forehead and added his head wouldn't need casting in bronze. He laughed a lot at his own joke.

A week later Levan met Tavzarashvili at a colleague's wedding reception. The tables were laid in the garden and most guests agreed the place looked like Eden. Academic Tavzarashvili remarked he couldn't bear to be among so many flowers as he was from Eastern Georgia, not particularly abundant in flowers.

"Oh, but you love roses," the host squinted jokingly.

"Roses? The rose was introduced into Georgia by the Persians. The lilac is our flower—it blossoms like a flame and dies down like a flame. As for Paradise, I'm going to have enough of it because I've already got a one-way ticket there."

"Stop it, Lado," the host protested. "Have you forgotten Rustaveli's words that no sensible man kills himself till Death."

"Yes, but where are the sensible people?" Tavzarashvili laughed. Then he remembered his mother, saying most of all he missed the young nettles prepared by her. When he married, he said, he took his wife to the village to meet his mother. She cooked nettles at his request and his wife whispered to him not to eat them because they'd sting him, he chuckled.

When the guests began to leave, Tavzarashvili stopped Levan and asked him if he remembered his visit to the clinic and how much he laughed there.

"There was nothing to laugh about. It was scary!" He stressed the last word, uttering it very loudly.

"You were scared? What of?" Levan asked.

"What was her name? That patient of yours?"

"Which patient?" Levan was unsure.

"I remember," Tavzarashvili said. "Her name is Nunu. God will never forgive me!" he added.

"I'm afraid I don't follow you," Levan was genuinely confused.

Tavzarashvili turned and headed for the gate. Then he stopped, looked back at Levan and said: "When I was standing at your father's monument, do you know what I was thinking about? I was thinking people were much kinder in the past ..."

The next time he saw Tavzarashvili was ten years later and from a distance. It was on the airfield when, together with others, Levan was getting into the plane flying to Sukhumi. The elderly man was standing in the middle of the field, surrounded by a pack of stray dogs, with a hat in his hand. They said since the day his son perished in the plane fire in Babushera, Tavzarashvili went to the airfield every single day and stood there with his head uncovered.

"As far as I recall, you were discharged quite soon, weren't you?" Levan asked the woman.

"In fact, I was transferred to another clinic. You weren't there when at midnight I was put in a car and driven away. Apparently you don't remember, but why should you anyway? I used to tell my story to everyone, including you of course, because you were in charge of my ward. Do you recall nothing, nothing at all?"

"Nothing except your name."

The woman opened another pack of cigarettes.

"You and I had just started our respective careers," she said with a smile, "you as a doctor, I as an insane patient. I'm tremendously grateful to you, first of all because you got me used to smoking ..."

"Who is ever thankful for that?" Levan laughed.

"Oh, I am. I can't imagine what I'd do if I didn't smoke. Secondly, I'm grateful that you're listening."

"That's nothing. Actually, it's my duty, especially since I was your ward doctor, wasn't I?"

"No, no! I don't want you to listen out of duty. I hate the word! It's awful, isn't it?"

"I'm not sure ..."

"So you disagree!"

Levan avoided answering her: "I believe you wanted to tell me something."

"No one wants to listen to anyone anymore," she said. "That's why they choose to watch TV. But there's so much you can hear from another person! Everyone knows and carries so much!"

"Sometimes unaware they know it," Levan smiled.

"Exactly. No one wants to listen anymore. They say they've got no time. But the world is full of time like a pool with water." She got to her feet, went over to Levan and stroked his hair. Levan didn't move. "And we delight in it, enjoying ourselves." She went back to her seat. "Just like dolphins, splashing and playing around. For some reason, I've always remembered you." She touched her scar. "Some considered this as a sign of madness, while I've never done anything as sane or as necessary as this. As I said, you heard my story in the clinic and heard it several times. And yet, I'm not at all surprised you've forgotten it. Actually, it would be surprising if you remembered it. I, on the other hand, was telling it practically without any variation for ten years, when asked or ordered to do so. What's more, I listened to the record with my own voice narrating it. I suppose some things, quite a few in fact, were my addition, the result of my disturbed mind. In short, my story is a mixture of reality, dreams, fantasy, thoughts, wishes and hopes, aspirations and images—my life made up by me. Much of it is the fruit of my imagination but the bulk of my story really happened to me. Sadly, from my bitter experience, I can't persuade anyone to believe it. Most of it was told by the Visitor—for practical reasons, let's call him the Visitor, the one who is the main character of my narrative. True, I didn't understand his language, but do people always make themselves understood solely through words? Because there are languages of eyes, hands, gestures, and even silence. Anyway, he managed to tell me enough to nurture my imagination to make up a myth about a man who came down from the sky. Yes, it is a myth!" she repeated with a smile. "And I'm its author, someone who gradually believed that everything narrated really happened to me. I'd like to add that the more I told the story, the more I was convinced the world was deaf. No one heard me. Quite recently I've typed it on the computer because I've taken a computer literacy course and thought it would be fun to have it written down. However, I don't cherish any hope that there are people out there who want to read it either. Okay, I'm joking. I'm not referring to you. I've brought this CD to you. If you have time, you might want to read it. For some reason I believe you'll find it interesting."

Levan took the CD.

"Sounds interesting..."

She interrupted him: "A lot of it is true!" She lit another cigarette. She sat with her eyes closed for quite some time, then said, "I don't want to leave!" She opened her eyes and added, "Are you scared?"

"Oh no! Why should I be?"

"Personally, if I were the Sultan, I'd have the chatterbox executed!"

"What chatterbox?" Levan wanted to know.

"Scheherazade!" she smiled. "But people are much kinder in fairy tales than in real life. Even me, didn't I tell my story over and over again just to preserve myself? I invented some of the details, added thing,s and then completely forgot which ones were true and which were made up. Actually, it doesn't matter in the least. I spent ten years in psychiatric clinics. It took me a long time to realize I wasn't merely a patient, but that I was a prisoner. I suddenly realized it in Moscow, where the clinic was full of dissidents, amazingly sensible and highly intelligent people..."

When she mentioned Scheherazade, Levan guessed her visit would be long or would become frequent. And he was right.

4

Nothing could be seen through the porthole except a red wall of meteorites. The control panel was twinkling in many colors, also indicating the trouble he was in. Among the hazards his people could face in open space, the meteorite cloud—this stomach of the cosmic pirates—was considered fatal because the Voice was lost. It was the Voice which directed the pilots' actions, teaching them what to do in times of trouble.

Suddenly the meteorites disappeared and he saw a cardioid planet, so called because of its resemblance to a heart. He was approaching it at a dangerous speed. His panel showed how he passed through the exosphere, ionosphere, mesosphere, and stratosphere until he fell into the troposphere. It was like taking a ride in a high speed lift. Almost immediately he felt his glass module hit the water and bob up and down. It was the Pacific Ocean. He travelled to nearly all parts of the planet, crisscrossed it in all directions till he ended up in Abastumani woods, the place, in Nunu's words, he was destined to be. You can't run away from your destiny, Nunu said. Thanks to the poor imagination of one of the witnesses, his module was dubbed the flying saucer. In fact, it could become completely weightless while moving, transform from its physical state into an aspiration, thus becoming as fast as an aspiration or a thought. In desperation it hit the invisible walls of the planet, unable to find the way out, the White Rabbit hole that would allow him to escape. The Earth seemed to have protective armor around it. Not only physical objects were bound to stay on the surface, even the radio waves failed to penetrate it, so perfect was the natural protection of this small planet unless one knew where exactly the escape door, hole, or crack was.

Now he lived in a cave in the woods and of course he had no idea the place was called Abastumani. He befriended a wolf. At night they used to sit at the cave opening, staring at the star-studded sky.

One day he saw a woman on the opposite slope. She was gathering mushrooms into the lap of her dress. That night he dreamt of her—she was standing wrapped in thick fog up to her chin, staring at something with a glazed look. He moaned and opened his eyes. A strange, hitherto unfelt melancholy gripped him. The next day the woman came to the same slope again. He headed towards her. Noticing him, she let go of her dress, dropping the mushrooms. He approached her and put his hand on her shoulder. She looked him directly in the eyes, without blinking, then rubbed her cheek against his hand. She turned and walked away. She came back two days later, bringing him a branch of a sycamore tree. They stood looking at each other, not uttering a word. Then he took her hand and led her into the cave ... When she left, he let loose a bloodcurdling cry directed towards the sky, as if trying to let his native planet know of his happiness. After that the woman came nearly every day.

From his module he had transferred everything he might need in the wood. Then he pushed it down the crevice to the bottom of the ravine. By then he had lost all hope of returning to his native planet despite the constant buzz the tag on his neck produced. Once the woman put her ear to the dog tag but, unable to hear anything except soft buzzing, looked at him questioningly. He said he would be found. He didn't offer any other explanation.

He was thinking about her, reclining on his side with his head propped on his arm. The wolf was sitting next to him. The lulled world around them was filled with silence complete with rustling, creaking, crackling, burbling, and warbling. Every world has its own specific silence. The buzzing of his dog tag seemed to intensify and alienate the silence which already sounded like music to his ears. It felt like listening to his own thoughts put into words: Tell me, tell me, why is it that I want to be alone and my loneliness isn't haunting me?

Unexpectedly, a little boy riding a donkey appeared on the path hidden in the lush shrubbery. Having descended from the sky, the man certainly didn't know the boy was the local ranger's son. The retarded boy used to take newspapers from the post-office to the observatory on the top of the mountain. Noticing the wolf, the donkey spun, tossed the boy and trotted down the hill, kicking all the way as if the wolf was chasing it. In truth, the wolf didn't even budge. Yelling for help, the boy ran after the donkey, as fast as he could ...

Some time later the woman came from the observatory and made for the cave. As she neared it, she halted, alarmed by the strangely tense silence — dead silence, in fact. Then she saw the dead man and the wolf at the mouth of the cave. The weirdest part was that she wasn't in the least surprised, as if she knew all along that she would find both the man and the wolf killed. She seemed to have reconciled with the idea ...

The very first time they met she guessed he wasn't local in the broadest sense of the word. That is to say he wasn't from this world. That's probably why she was gripped with the fear of death from day one. But she didn't know who was to die — she, having seen the Visitor, or the Visitor, squatting, patting the wolf lying at his feet. The beast's death didn't count because it didn't compare to her own or the Visitor's death. It was precisely the feeling or dread of death that sped up everything which happened between them. Like a silent melody, the shadow of death accompanied and intensified their passionate attraction to each other, which was all-consuming as it was. The way she saw it, their entwined bodies wheeled down the slope at a frightening speed, leaving a singing blood trail on the blade-sharp stones. Afterwards, they seemed to struggle back, laboriously climbing the slope, freeing themselves from the entangling haze holding them like thorny bramble, finally lying side by side like a pair of fish tossed onto the beach by the waves, able to survive only if the very same wave returned them back to their natural element ...

She felt it wasn't only her secret. It could have become an omen of a global catastrophe. In a way, being a scientist, precisely an astronomer, it even obliged her to report to the relevant authorities the location of the man from space, but ... She couldn't take that step. It was more than she could bear. She shuddered at the thought that the man she betrayed in this way would fall victim to the cruelty of science — a guinea pig that is never asked if it finds it fun when it's skinned alive. She felt rather acutely she was making a mistake, betraying first of all her own profession. Something she sought out during the hours spent looking through the observatory telescope was right there, beside her on Earth. But the problem was that the outer space Visitor had become part of her essence, which drew her to him with a powerful craving to become one. She was drawn to him, attracted and pulled like an animated shred of paper escaping the blaze, yearning to turn into a new flame even if for a very short while.

She took the dog tag off the dead. Put it into her pocket. That was when she heard panting. Someone was scrambling up the slope. She hid behind a tree. It was the ranger. He had a spade and a pick-axe over one shoulder and a rifle over the other. He was heading directly towards the cave. He dropped the spade and the pickaxe on the ground, leaned his rifle against the tree and sat on a boulder. He lit a cigarette. She came from behind the tree.

"Did you kill him?" she asked.

The ranger didn't answer. He got to his feet and spit on the palms of his hands. With the blade of his spade he drew a rectangle on the ground. Then he picked up his pickaxe. She went nearer.

"Are you going to kill me too?"

He ignored her again.

That's how they were for a long time—him digging, her watching. Strange but she didn't even think of running away. Probably because, even if she tried, she wouldn't be able to run away from the ranger. Then she said: "Give me the spade. I'll help you."

He immediately passed her the spade. He was standing knee-deep in the grave. He climbed out and lit a cigarette.

For quite a while they took turns digging. Then they threw the corpses into the grave and covered them with soil. The ranger broke branches from the nearby shrubs and threw them over the new grave. Then he picked them up and tossed them away. Instead, he cut squares of turf from different places and put them side by side on the newly filled grave. Now it was undistinguishable from the rest of the area.

"You look experienced," she said. He didn't reply.

Then they sat down again.

"And who did you kill?" he asked.

Now it was her turn not to answer. She leaned back, resting her head on her hands, and stared at the blue patches of sky seen through the foliage. She heard a cuckoo from afar as if it were her own heart that went: cu-ckoo, cu-ckoo.

It might be better this way, a much better option, she thought. But she didn't make any effort to think why this death was a better option ...

Most of all I loved Brueghel. I used to read Brueghel's album as a book of poems. I would keep it by my bed and leaf though it before I fell asleep. The strange visions that started in my younger days might have been intensified by the imagination of the great Dutchman to such an extent that sometimes I found it hard to differentiate whether something was happening in reality or was the result of my imagination. The lewdest image that haunted me was a little nobody in a doublet—a typical Brueghel character—screwing an enormous moon. You might have easily guessed the image was influenced by Brueghel's *Flemish Proverbs*, specifically from the picture in which a spread-legged scoundrel is pissing at the moon (or its reflection). What else but a proverb can better render the idea that humans apparently don't deserve the world so generously given by the Almighty because they are certainly unable to appreciate the Great Wonder? It was the symbolic image of ungrateful mankind. But my visions didn't stop there: the little nobody would turn to face me, grinning and flashing his fleshy legs, and expose his penis. Sensual hallucinations kept tormenting me, weird scenes strangely connected to each other.

We slept in a king-size bed. Due to a surgical mistake my husband was unable to have normal intercourse so we helped each other. A masturbating couple. And all the while that little nobody, the Brueghel creature, used to tear me apart like a brute, drag me down the barren ground, and I would leave my flesh on the shrubs, brambles, and rocks. I seemed to resist him, fight back, but in fact it was my struggle that excited him more. He would rip my clothes off, bite my nipples, tear at my underwear with his teeth. I screamed and groaned and whined. A kind of beastly, wickedly dark orgasm used to blot out my mind. Instead of coming, I used to feel drained out. Then suddenly I'd come to my senses, start catching my breath, spared and petrified, wrapped in a soaking nightie fit to be wrung out. My husband lay next to me, covering his head with a blanket. Of course he was awake, of course he was aware of what was going on, but it was obvious, was it? He never let me know though, not even a word. Only once, I'm not sure in what connection, he muttered more to himself: "The monastery charter didn't consider it a sin if monks ejaculated in their sleep." That was that ...

I was an astrophysicist, my husband a writer, spending all his days at the typewriter. I used to go over to him, lean on his shoulders with my elbows and read what he had been typing. These were easily the most idyllic moments in our married life but it's only fair to say that it was love that made me marry a man twenty-five years my senior, someone I'd loved since my schooldays. Better to say I had loved what he wrote. At night I'd fall asleep pressing his book to my heart. In my dreams I'd turn into one of his characters, someone thirsty for love, gripped by an eerie melancholy. Once I bragged to my friends that I'd marry him one day. And I did! But that was later, when I already graduated from the university. I visited him. It was a surprise to him. He didn't remember me. Why would he if he'd seen me only once? He had been invited to the university to talk to a group of young aspiring writers. I had approached him with his book and asked him to sign it. He asked my name. And all the while I believed he'd remember me, even consider me very special. That time I stayed at his place for a long time. We talked and talked till quite late. Then everything happened in a banal way. No, actually there was nothing banal about it. It was anything but banal, especially that he was unable to have traditional intercourse for instance. I found it surprising but didn't show it. I said it didn't matter to me when he asked how I felt about it. I laughed saying I wasn't a virgin, adding I'd accumulated quite a lot of experience for my twenty-two years. I lied. I had no experience whatsoever. I wasn't a virgin though. A guy I knew managed to take care of that in the bathroom at a friend's birthday party. Then he disappeared, apparently terrified of the consequences.

Upon completion of my doctoral degree, I was sent to the Abastumani Observatory. My husband followed me. He said it was immaterial where he lived, even thought the place would be better. We had no strings attached: his mother died just before we moved, and my mother had moved in with her new husband.

We brought everything we might have needed to the cottage allocated to us. The amount of luggage was truly amazing. We just couldn't discard our old things from our old houses, especially the books. Now I think we suffered from human nostalgia, a lack of human vitamins which not only we but several generations sought to compensate through reading. I had the impression my husband had read everything there was to read. Mainly he enjoyed the Roman poets, particularly Catullus who he read more often than others. He even intended to translate his poems and learned Latin for the purpose. Books, you may easily agree, are heavy to carry, especially when they're part of your baggage. The same applies to art albums and vinyl records. We also brought lots of cassettes. Ultimately, it meant I could listen to my favorite music whenever I chose to, for instance Grieg's piano concerto performed by Richter. Not only do I like Scandinavian music and literature, but thinking about Scandinavia miraculously calms me down. It has the same effect on me as an attic full of magic things for a dreamy child. But isn't Scandinavia kind of the magic attic of Europe?

Our little flat was soon full of books — they were on the shelves, tables, floor, and window sills. In our sitting room — the largest room in our tiny house — we hung a Khevsurian rug on the wall with my husband's double barreled hunting gun and the ammunition belt. We even had a small fireplace. In front of it we spread a bear skin bought from a local gamekeeper. We used to lie on it and stare at the flames. "Pensive at the hearth, like Dickens' characters", as one of our poets said. My husband would mostly be quiet while I talked. He dropped a phrase or two if he agreed with what I said, but frowned if he didn't. When I felt I was overdoing it, I'd stop, saying I was tired of talking. "No", he used to say, "keep talking, I like it when you talk." Usually I protested, saying I did a lot of talking as it was, mainly on the phone of course. Having a land-line phone was a huge privilege, an expression of respect towards my husband demonstrated by the local government. It was 1980, too early for cell phones ...

"Look at the son of a bitch! He's pissing at the moon!" I shouted, striking the picture with the back of my hand.

"You always react with the same fury," my husband smiled. "Every time you look at the picture, you are angry, as if he's going to stop it."

"I'd kill the rogue with pleasure. Have your cigarette here if you wish, don't go," I told him. We were reclining on the bear skin by the fireplace.

"You can't stand the smoke, can you?"

"That's okay. I want to tell you something." I could no longer keep back the truth from him.

I had been seeing the man from the sky for some time. Had my husband been healthy, surely I'd have told him earlier. It might have been his condition that stopped me from telling the truth. Actually, not might, it certainly was.

"Okay, I won't smoke," he said. "I'm listening."

"It's nothing," I patted his knee.

After a while I said:

"You know, my profession failed to make me a good astronomer but managed to make an amateur philosopher out of me. Want to hear what I'm thinking about when I stare through the telescope? It's inane, but I'm still going to tell you: astronomy is nothing else but our nostalgia over the lost paradise."

"Not sure about a philosopher but you're certainly a poet," my husband said with a smile.

"Possibly, and I like that even better! It kind of suits me more. I know you don't like it when I prattle, but you've got to be patient. You've got no choice and can't sneak out." All the while I was stroking his hand, his beautifully slender fingers. I used to laugh, he had the idle fingers of a writer. In fact it was these long fingers that worked day and night, typing, day in day out, tirelessly hitting the keys. As a result he looked like a hermit. And not only looked like one, but actually was one. He never mentioned it but I felt he had escaped something truly unpleasant when he chose to leave Tbilisi. That's why I consciously avoided talking about literature, I mean our modern writing.

I had never thought about whether my husband loved me or not. I just assumed that he did. It took me two years to start doubting. Why should he love a girl who so suddenly appeared in his life, pressing his book to her chest and meekly asking for his autograph in a quivering voice? They say you can't cheat destiny. That's exactly what happened to us — my husband and I were destined to be together without any prerequisite, without even considering it necessary to get to know each other better. I was stunned by my own boldness but at the same time I was aware I was imitating one of his characters, her manner of talking and moving. Except I couldn't get used to smoking. I tried but nearly choked. I suspect he saw through me because once he said with a smile that I was a better girl than I thought. By then we were already seeing each other, or rather I used to visit him. He lived with his elderly mother, forever neatly combed and dressed as if ready to go out. The thin, grey-haired woman used to sit in front of the TV, and never talked to me. She would glance at me, nod slightly, and turn back to the screen. I was sure she couldn't overhear our conversation but, frankly speaking, I tended to forget there was someone else in the room apart from the two of us. It looked as if Beso, my future husband, was reluctant to take me to the other room or to indicate, somehow hint with his eyes, that we weren't alone. That must have been the reason he nodded to everything I said with a polite smile. But there was no stopping me, as if I felt I wouldn't be able to find a more appreciative listener. It was him I absolutely had to tell about my thoughts and feelings or which book or film I fancied. And not only that—

I used to recite lengthy passages from his book! He listened with his head dropped down. In general, he wasn't much of a talker, or it might have seemed so, especially compared to me. Once we went for a walk. At Anchiskhati Church we sat on the low stone wall and I suggested going inside. We lit candles. I told him to make a wish. I certainly did and it came true! A couple of days later when we were talking in his sitting room as usual, he leaned towards me, put his hand on mine, and asked if I'd marry him. That's when I was lost for words. I just stared at him. He was worried, wondering if it came totally unexpectedly. I didn't answer. Then he turned to his mother: "Mum, this is my future wife." Her expression didn't change. Only later I caught a glimpse of her reflection in the TV screen, spotting a glint of a tear in her eye ... The next day he told me the story of his fatal operation. We were buying the wedding rings. He was so calm and matter-of-fact that for a second I even thought he was punishing me for my audacity. In general, God always mocks me by fulfilling all my wishes but in the weirdest, most unimaginable ways. We were getting our rings, but in fact I knew nothing about him, except of course his books. I didn't know because I didn't want to, chose to turn a deaf ear to his numerous romantic adventures I heard from my friends and acquaintances, who kept narrating them as if deliberately. I had resolved he was to start a new life with me, and that's exactly what happened ...

I spent every single spare minute walking in the woods. I had hiked every hill and mountain, visited every small village, crossed every field and meadow. I preferred walking alone, shunning company during these long walks. My husband loved staying at home and writing, and of course listening to music, especially the German Romantic composers. "Stop these solitary walks," the locals warned me over and over again. There were plenty of thugs and sexually disturbed patients from the nearby TB sanatorium roaming the area, they reasoned with me. I was warned against possible trouble but actually I came across a miracle, a true wonder. A huge celestial drop emanating heavenly light from his body which had taken a human shape. It was the first time I felt what the sky was, saw it for the first time. Not for a moment did I think he might have been an alien, mainly because he was no different from us. Most of all he was utterly dissimilar to all the hideous aliens from all the science fiction films, the ones swaying like seaweeds, hardly holding their pumpkin-like heads on thin necks. I won't recount what happened between us later because I don't wish to repeat myself. The only thing I'm going to say is it was the first time I fully appreciated how wonderful it was to be a woman! Till then I'd never had normal intercourse in my life. The most disgusting time was that one in the bathroom which left me with the repulsive sensation of wetness and cold. I remember sitting on the edge of the bath tub for a while, feeling tired, completely drained, and utterly surprised for some reason. And all the while I felt that not only the recent sickening experience, but everything else too, was senseless. I locked myself in. Turned on the hot water. Found the shampoo. I undressed and soaked myself in stinking rather than aromatic bubbles. I closed my eyes. Must have dozed off. I was brought to my senses by loud banging on the door. Finally I came out of the bathroom. "Were you taking a bath?" the girls asked me. "Have you gone insane?" I said yes and asked for a drink . . .

I met the man from the sky a few times. Of course I didn't run to our rendezvous like Emma Bovary but I couldn't imagine not going to see him. Most worryingly, I couldn't tell anyone about my sensational secret, the significance of which, or rather the enormity of it, dawned on me only gradually. We both very quickly adopted the obvious and the easiest, the speech of live hieroglyphics—the language of the mute. After that the gigantic secret shrank, only to become my private one. God seemed to encourage me by saying that what I'd thought about the universe and its inhabitants was correct. But most importantly, I saw the creature embodying the infinite, and not only saw, but actually perceived him. Once again I was convinced that, just like the universe, a human is a world of infinity. The intelligent life scattered across boundless space is no different from a human, from us . . .

It was early autumn. As I said, I used to spend my free time walking in the woods and fields, thinking about numerous things, silly ideas churning in my head. Oddly, a line from a poem kept popping up again and again: "And all becomes so gentle around." I even repeated the line aloud. Indeed, the area was strangely gentle, softly silenced. Cobwebs glistened among the branches. And I seemed to be wrapped in a soft, sun-warmed net, like a helpless insect unaware of the deadly peril. It instinctively accepts death as inevitable, knows that it's bound to happen. The foliage is immersed in the peaceful, self-assured tranquility, smugly still, boasting of colors, forever changing the hues. It looks pretty stable but soon the dazzling autumn striptease will start. At times, just like a drop of water on the tap rim, a leaf will detach itself from the branch, come spinning, sliding, gliding in the air, dancing to the music unheard by us, fully succumbing to its rhythm. It's still alive, or thinks it's alive, but is now alone, solitary, left on its own, not part of the myriad of its kin any longer, just a tiny part of the green darkness created by the myriad of its kind. Slightly upset and frightened by this sudden realization, it keeps flying and dancing, somewhat astonished and dazzled though. In short, it doesn't know it's free and dies. It spins for some time but then, as if suddenly becoming heavier, starts to fall—sliding towards the ground, spreading itself on the earth. That's how it finishes its life with a soft touchdown—dancing to the end. I was thinking that morning: Does it have to be a leaf to teach us that one death forewarns of many more to follow? Somehow grown and strangely transformed by the news, which I even had checked with the doctor of the local clinic, I was unhurriedly walking home, dizzy with the inexplicable happiness I couldn't fully realize. What the doctor confirmed should have been a true disaster given my personal life. But, lo and behold! It was the other way round: thousands of shiny and glittering beads of joy kept spinning in my head. And not only in my head. My whole body was bustling as if fireworks had been let loose, as if it had turned into a shred of the sky, into a new territory of the sky. Only, of course, if it's at all possible to imagine the swelling and growth of the sky.

I began to walk faster, thinking I should share my joy with my husband. I didn't have other people I could call close and wasn't particularly friendly with my colleagues. Then I got angry with myself: "Are you out of your mind? Don't even think about it!" True. If there was one person I couldn't tell about it, worst of all expect to get thrilled by it, it was my husband. Suddenly I noticed a lot of people around, among them many soldiers. Something was amiss, something unusual must have happened, otherwise why were they here, what were they looking for? But I couldn't ask anybody. Immediately I was reminded of the grave near the cave. Then I saw the ranger.

"Carlo!" I called him. "Come here!"

He came over to me. Slowly, reluctantly, moving with deliberation. He kept looking around as if unwilling to be seen with me.

"What's going on?" I asked. "Who are they? What are they looking for?"

"They found it," he said quietly, avoiding my eyes.

"What?" my heart thumped.

"The geologists have found it. At the bottom of the ravine."

"Found what? What could there be in the ravine?"

"Something. I'm not sure what. Pardon, lady, but I nearly shit myself with fear."

I sighed with relief.

"Don't worry," I said. "Be a man!"

"I rely on you," Carlo said and gazed away.

"Don't be afraid. I've told you I'm dumb as a gravestone."

"A lot of army around, more and more trucks are arriving."

"Don't be scared," I told him again and left.

My husband was typing. He didn't even raise his head when I went into the room. I hung my jacket on the rack. Took off my sneakers, leaving them by the wardrobe. I crossed the room in my socks, stroked his hair and asked how things were going. He didn't reply.

"It's so nice outside!"

He nodded. It didn't matter to him what was happening outside.

He was uninterested.

"Such a lot of people! And soldiers too. I wonder what's going on."

"I know," he said and stopped typing. He stretched his arms. "I'm tired. They phoned me offering a walk in the woods. Must've needed more people."

"Why aren't you going then? Nothing better than a leisurely walk in the woods—it's so beautiful! If I were you, I'd take the gun and go. Remember Baudelaire? 'I took my gun and went out to kill time.'"

He smiled: "Why would I need the gun?"

"I don't know. But you're its proud owner, aren't you?"

"It's my dad's gun."

"Fine, but does it matter? Doesn't it shoot if it's your dad's? You do clean and polish it regularly. Who or what are they looking for? Did they tell you?"

"Said they found something in the ravine."

"Such as?"

"Something … How do I describe it? Something like a spacecraft. I don't believe it. Sounds like a sci-fi film!"

And something strange happened—I was offended, can you imagine? Deeply offended but to this very day I'm not sure what was it that hurt me. Was it that he called my happiness, the joy that completely filled me, sci-fi? Possibly that's why I changed my mind about keeping it a secret and blurted out: "I'm pregnant!"

He was taken aback.

He stared at me for a long time.

I immediately knew I shouldn't have told him but it was too late.

Without a single word he turned to his typewriter and hit the keys …

The next day, as soon as I came back from the observatory and opened the door, an unusual silence made me uneasy. I remember thinking it was unusual … He had the double-barreled hunting gun pressed to his chest, his big toe still on the trigger …

It wasn't a scream. An abominable creature seemed to be ready to jump out of my mouth. I covered it with both hands. I stood there for a long time. Then went onto the balcony and took the canister. I sprinkled the paraffin around the room. Emptied the can and dropped it in the corner. From the cupboard I took a bottle of Cuban rum, which I had brought from Tbilisi. Sat in the armchair and drank straight from the bottle. Felt like swallowing fire. I got to my feet. Went to the kitchen to fetch matches. Then returned to the armchair. Took another swig. This time I kind of liked it. I struck the match. Stared at it for a short while as if it was a beetle on a pin, then tossed it and took another swig, a larger one. I started to sing. Quite unexpectedly for myself. It was a simple song from my childhood. I was singing and drinking and all the while tears ran down my cheeks. Because of the smoke. I was choking on it, coughing, my eyes were burning, but I kept singing ...

I opened my eyes in a hospital ward. The first thing I saw was a young bald man with a white coat over his shoulders. I managed to ask what the date was. My mouth was dry and my lips were swollen. The young man replied with a smile I should have asked about the month rather than the day. I immediately blacked out, but not because of his words. Before I opened my eyes again, I was dreaming I was in the Abastumani woods. With its eyes half-closed, the wolf had its head in my lap. "Where's your friend?" I asked it, scratching it behind the ears. "Can't you see him?" it asked. I said I couldn't. I felt he was there, somewhere near me, probably even in me. That's why I cried. And that's when I woke up or came to my senses or came back to life—not sure what to call it. And I immediately saw the same bald young man. He was staring at me exactly as he did before my blackout. I learned from him that I had been in a coma-like state for five months. The next day two of his colleagues brought a recorder into the ward and let me listen to my own delirious speech for more than an hour. It turned out that in my sleep, or whatever the state was, I talked continuously about the man who came from the sky.

"Can you hear?" the bald man asked me.

I nodded.

"Can you recognize your voice?"

I nodded again. He didn't make it a secret that he was an intelligence officer. During the whole five months, he had been sitting by my bed, waiting for me to wake up or rather come back to life. And, of course, had been recording whatever I said. I spoke clearly and calmly as if I knew it was taped. Interestingly, I was repeating the same story, without any striking variations.

"So," the major said, "you're repeating the same thing over and over again."

I replied after a long pause: "I'm telling my husband all that happened," and added, "I've never lied to him."

"Your husband is dead," the major said.

I couldn't help it. Tears streaked down my face, burning the skin on my neck.

"I know," I said quietly.

I remembered everything all too clearly. What baffled me was how I got out of it alive, who saved me, how I got to the hospital. In fact, I didn't want to be saved. I wasn't at all ready to start a new life. As I listened to my voice, I was surprised at my own calmness. Moreover, I was bewildered by the weird precision, the pedantic accuracy of the text which I was repeating just like a recorded message.

The major got to his feet and wiped my tears with a tissue. That's when I realized I couldn't move a finger. I was bandaged like a mummy.

"Is your story true?" the major asked smiling kindly.

I nodded.

"Can you tell me now what happened?"

After a long while I replied: "No."

"Why's that?"

"I'm tired."

He immediately sprang up and addressed someone sitting behind him: "Take care of her!"

The next day I narrated my story to him word for word, exactly as it was recorded on the tape.

For some time he sat quietly, then said:

"Please be frank with me, did you invent that fairy tale?"

"A tale?"

If my narrative was considered a piece of fiction, why did he spend all those months by my bed? Or why did they look after me so carefully; why did they support life in my practically dead body? Why was I brought back to life from what must have been a clinical death?

He seemed to have guessed my thoughts. He smiled with his strange lopsided smile—only his lips stretched. He looked away and said, as if to himself:

"Do you actually understand the meaning of your story?"

Then he drew a piece of paper from the case at his feet. He stared at it for a long time. I believe he wasn't reading it, just playing for time before saying:

"A physicist!"

I replied: "I haven't held anything back. Even from the person I should've told nothing. Yes, I am a physicist, an astronomer. And I understand perfectly well what I've said."

"All the more!" he said.

That day we didn't talk anymore.

When I woke up the next morning he was sitting by my bed again.

"Of course," I said, "some things, actually a lot of things, are added, purely my inclusion, but the main point is we were really seeing each other."

"And you ..."

"He was an alien!"

"But why ..."

"Didn't I notify the authorities?"

Our conversation began to resemble a game—I had to guess what he wanted to say. So far I was doing fine.

"I didn't because ..."

I stopped, as if suggesting he join in, and he readily followed the rules of the game: "You fell in love with him."

Until that moment I was talking to him but not looking at him. Now I turned my head. He wasn't smiling, his face tense, a bead of sweat glistening on his temple.

"How do you know?" I asked.

"Because you're pregnant!" He blurted it out severely, even rudely.

I suddenly remembered about my pregnancy.

"I've got a husband!" I tried to protest.

"You had one," he corrected me calmly.

Apparently, he was well informed, including my husband's problems.

I said after a short pause: "I haven't held back anything. That recording is absolutely true. It all happened like that. And I can't add anything. Now, can I ask you leave me alone? I'm very weak."

Without another word, he got to his feet and left.

That night I went into premature labor. It might not have been premature but that's what I believed. I didn't even know how long I'd been in hospital, how much time had passed since ... At that point I stopped thinking, because recalling the past was excruciating. When I felt the pain, I was somehow relieved because it'd save me from the annoyingly polite talk with the investigator.

Strangely enough, I felt no connection with the baby except the pain when it came out of my body like a rough piece of rock. No, that was my imagination, or rather that's how I perceived the pain in my imagination because the baby was born by Caesarian section and I was heavily anesthetized. Surely, they brought it to show me but I didn't even look. "A girl, it's a girl" was all I heard. I just couldn't look at her. Milk was oozing from my swollen breasts. They hurt. I was well aware I had a baby but that was it. Believe it or not, I had no emotion towards her. Not surprisingly, I had no wish to see her. That's no good, the doctors used to reprimand me, it's your baby after all. They found it bewildering. So, it can be said that I did have a baby but failed to become a mother.

Soon I was able to get up. I was allowed into the hall. I used to shuffle along the corridor all alone. The wards on that floor were empty. Then came a new investigator. He was holding a bunch of flowers as if it were a signal flag. They were, how do I put it, kind of official flowers, the type that haven't got names, only numbers. He was wearing plain clothes but apparently couldn't find a matching tie, so he had a khaki one, the kind they wear with a uniform and that fastens at the neck with a button.

"Do you feel better?" he asked.

"Thank you. I'm fine."

"Oh, sorry," he shoved rather than gave me the flowers. "Congratulations on having a baby."

I thanked him. Put the flowers on the window sill. Immediately the nurse came in, put the flowers in a glass jar and placed it on the table. She stared at the investigator. He indicated she could go. The nurse closed the door quietly behind her. I knew all his questions by heart. He didn't ask anything new, however, unlike the previous investigator, he accused me of treason. He did smile, but his expression remained unchanged. I laughed: "If it's treason, probably it's better to blame me for betraying the planet rather than my country!"

Just like the previous one, this officer also brought in the cassette player and made me listen to my delirious prattle again. It went on for several days. Eventually, he told me I was being transferred to another clinic the following day. Which one, I asked. Wasn't this a clinic? Psychiatric, he replied calmly and immediately added: "Is it so unexpected?"

"Can I be frank?"

"Sure! That's why I'm here."

"I thought you'd hit me."

"How can you say that? What made you even think of it!" he sounded genuinely surprised, even affronted.

"Why am I being transferred to the psychiatric clinic? Am I mad?"

"What you've been saying," he indicated the tape with his gaze, "and what you actually did ..."

"Oh my god," I sighed.

"Yes," he went on, "can all this be considered normal?"

"How do you know what is normal and what is abnormal?" I exclaimed, rather argumentatively, which surprised me a lot. "How can you be so sure?" I shouted at him.

Without as much as raising his eyebrow, he replied evenly: "The experts will shed light on that issue."

"Including the treason?" I was extremely agitated. The mention of the clinic deeply upset me. The enormity of my misfortune seemed to dawn on me only now.

"That as well," he said and rose to his feet. He took the white coat hanging on the back of the chair. Unlike the previous investigator, he didn't bother to even wrap it around himself. When he came, he had it in his hand, trailing it behind. Soon I was transferred to the psychiatric clinic.

That day you woke up earlier than usual though it was Sunday and you could have enjoyed sleeping in. The previous day your former patient had brought an invitation—one of the foreign embassies was celebrating their national day. The event was scheduled for seven o'clock in the summer garden of the concert hall. The invitation said the presence of the honorable guest was desirable. If not for your former patient, you wouldn't have considered going because you became 'honorable' only thanks to that patient! The bedroom window was ajar and you were shaving with an electric razor, looking in a little mirror on the window sill. You were talking to a bird sitting nearby, knocking on the tin ledge with its beak. You tried very hard to tell the bird how much you sympathized with it, but it wasn't very clear why that tiny creature deserved your pity. I believe you were wondering about it too. Not only the bird but everything around you—including your past and future life—seemed miserable. Possibly because you suddenly came to the realization that there aren't many things in the world as bitter and perturbing as the perception of yourself and your life separately, taken independently of each other. You must have thought that the time passes and drags you along as if you were a wounded soldier. But not to the infirmary. Time doesn't know an infirmary exists, but it does have a single address ... Neither knocking on the door nor unexpected phone calls startled you any longer. Nothing tensed you anymore, no unforeseen events scared you because you were well aware that anything that happened wasn't unexpected. Isn't that true? There is no such thing as unexpectedness ... Except words! That's what you really dread. Words are ruthless, mainly due to their unpredictability ...

Over there, beyond the open door there was the sitting room. The cleaning lady, who came twice a week, had switched on the TV. The two-story house that your grandfather had built was quite big. It even had a small garden in front with an iron fence and a little gate in it.

It wasn't the first time you went to such a party. Several times you had received the invitations personally, not surprisingly, as you were the head of a reputable clinic. Such clinics are particularly respected by foreigners and not without a good reason. Most frequently of course you were invited by the Swiss Embassy. Probably because you had spent ten years working there.

As a rule, these parties attract lots of people. It's a question of "prestige", in the modern vernacular. They try to turn up at the functions where, again borrowing a modern term, "the public faces" are bound to be in abundance. The majority of the guests are acquaintances of the Georgian staff. Incidentally, the invitation itself is also pretty prestigious. Once you saw one framed, hanging on the wall of someone you know. On the whole, the more prestigious things one owns—position, apartment, summer house, car, or lover—the more one is respected in and out of home, particularly by the media.

Clearly, it was the ten years spent in a free country that taught you to fully comply with the law if you want to live freely. On the one hand this sounds like an absurd condition, worthy of a sneer, unless one considers the fact that social and political laws and regulations are seldom based on logic and common sense. On the other hand, that's how they preserve their plausibility.

All this you wrote that morning in your diary, but when you finished, you automatically leafed through it and came across your own strange entry which was so different from others that could have been written by someone else: in the scorching, vast yellow desert a camel trudges, jingling its numerous bells. The camel is followed by the entire population of the planet—mankind in a miniscule typeface! The mass of teeny-weeny humans follows the camel like the shadow of a cloud ... Then one fine day, famished mankind killed and ate the camel. However, it was the camel that knew how to get them out of the desert, how to reach the oasis ... "What's this?" you thought. How could I have written it? Doesn't look like my writing at all! Doesn't sound like me either. What does this camel mean? Desert? Oasis? Mankind turned into a shadow of a cloud?

Could I too have eaten the camel and that's what saved me? You asked yourself these questions but were smiling all along: "Curious, my dear gentleman, curious." Then you looked at the date: 2001. The beginning of the new millennium! You were still in Switzerland but were dying to go back home. Was it only your nostalgic sentiments that made you picture the global catastrophe of humankind?

You finished shaving. Went into your study. The diary on the desk was open on the page with the camel story.

"Dear Sigmund," you addressed Freud's picture, that your dad had hung long ago in the most prominent place. Wonder what he thought at the time. "Dear guru, here I am, your colleague from Georgia, who saved money to get to Vienna from Switzerland like a Muslim to Mecca because I was thrilled with the poetry and esoteric mystery hidden in your works. However, I'd like to take the liberty to say that you never felt it despite admitting the dictate of the transcendental in creativity. At that time, I, a young man dazzled by your unprecedented courage, didn't notice or stop to think that you actually considered it possible to solve the mystery of the irrational impetus. Dare I say it, not every move of a human soul can be subjected to a psychiatrist's treatment or explanation. Because the moment we assume it's possible, a human as a mystery as such will cease to be. It took me quite a while to conclude that your arguments, dear guru, resembled those of an eloquent lawyer rather than the well-grounded argumentation of a scientist or a doctor. That's when I had this sacrilegious idea (I beg your pardon for it): you lack the ability to perceive the mysterious, which is paramount in order to be more plausible. I'm fully aware that for such heresy I deserve to be burnt at the stake in front of your clinic in Vienna, witnessed by thousands of psychiatrist tourists. But I can't help it—I still hold the conviction that not everything can be explained. 'There are more things in heaven and earth, Horatio ...' Besides, is it so necessary to find an explanation for everything around us? Suppose we do, what then? What do we do? Slay the camel that leads us to the oasis?"

It was the moan of a man, a tiny particle of the cloud shadow, burdened with age-old problems and subdued by doubts, who found himself on the threshold of a new epoch—2001, a new year, a new century, a new millennium …

She was standing at the long table with bottles and sandwiches. She was holding an empty wine glass in one hand and pushing a tress of hair from her forehead with two fingers of the other, as if giving a military salute. I thought she was smiling at me. Did I know her? I took a hesitant step towards her. No, I never met her. If I had, I'd remember. When I got nearer, I realized she was smiling at her own thoughts. She seemed far away, lost in her own world, unaffected by the din of the place crowded with guests. She was oblivious to her surroundings.

"Hello," I said in French. She definitely was a foreigner.

"What did you say?" she was jolted from her reverie. "Oh, sorry. Hello. Have we met?"

"Unfortunately, no. Would you like a drink?" I indicated the glass she was holding.

"No," she handed me the glass, "thanks." She walked away leaving me with it.

She was wearing a plain long, sleeveless dress with a deep cut at the back. Her step was light, her back very straight. Sliding like a sail. She stopped to talk to a man, with her back to me. The garden was quite full. Having just finished his long, boring speech, the Ambassador looked relieved, walking around with a broad smile followed by a group of ladies. He looked like a pale-skinned African if such a thing is possible to imagine. He was wearing a white suit with a bright red tie. I looked around trying to find my former patient, the one who sent me the invitation. I just wanted him to see I was there. Instead, I collided with the same tall woman.

"I'm looking for you," she said.

"Are you?" I was speechless.

"I'm Ana-Maria. Sorry for abandoning you."

"Don't worry," I was a bit confused. "Nice to meet you." I told her who I was.

"Can I excuse myself? I need to tend to the guests," she stretched out her hand. For some reason I held her hand in both of mine. I'd never done that before. She freed her hand with a smile. Moved away. Surprisingly, I immediately regretted having come to the party. The phrase began to haunt me: "Shouldn't have come, shouldn't have come." I went to the counter, took a glass of wine, drank it in a gulp. Then another and yet another … Shouldn't have come. I wasn't sure why I thought so. I felt awfully hot. Became dizzy. Hadn't had wine for a long time. Probably lost the habit. Could it be that my horrible disease which had tortured me for months was back? What if … What if … I sat down. Little by little my heartbeat calmed down. I went to the counter again and took another glass. This time I drank in small gulps. I was absolutely calm. Everything seemed to fall back to normal. I looked around but didn't see a single familiar face. I left the party. Nerves, nerves, nerves! You've got to take care of your nerves, you fool! I scolded myself …

A month lapsed after that. I'd nearly forgotten about the party, especially since I was extremely busy at the clinic and the research institute as well, with its ridiculous selection process. The weirdest one was selecting the staff on the basis of their age. Inexplicably, no one said anything against me though some quite eminent academics of my age, namely over fifty, were asked to leave their posts. In fact, I had resolved to resign because as an acting director, I found myself involved in issues that had either never interested me or were not within my scope of competence. It was better to leave and the sooner the better. Watching *The Saturday Comedy Show* with the livid faces of the anchors didn't help either. That was topped by a sweetly smiling official who talked like the police chief. I listened to him a couple of times and resolved not to go to the planned meeting with him because I guessed it was completely useless. He wouldn't have listened to my arguments anyway. But I still met him at a party launching yet another company. Unexpectedly I found myself face to face with this high-ranking official. And it must have been the unexpectedness that made me pour all I had to say right into his face. He was smiling throughout my emotional speech, indicating to someone behind me not to interfere. Of course, of course, of course was all he said before running away. Looking at the people around, all of a sudden I felt like a condemned officer whose shoulder straps had been unceremoniously ripped off, stripping him of his honor. Nothing mattered anymore—neither the academic degrees nor the number of publications. Apparently the only valuable asset was an ironic smile and fanatically bright eyes on the TV screen. I'd been scared of fanatics all my life, especially those who assumed fanaticism only to gain more from the ruling group. I regretted talking to him at all.

Time passed. The worst thing was that I couldn't read though it was exactly the moment when I needed the imaginary world most of all, especially since I'd always maintained that it was much more humane than the reality. Frankly speaking, our life is humane only in books.

I had just gone to bed and was about to turn the light off when the phone rang. I checked the time. It was one in the morning. I picked up the phone.

"Hello."

"Is that you, Levan?" a man asked me in French.

"Speaking."

"You were our guest quite recently."

"Excuse me?"

"At the garden party."

"Oh, yes, sure."

"I'm the First Secretary of the Embassy."

"What can I do for you?"

"Sorry to bother you so late."

"That's okay. You didn't wake me up."

"I'm afraid I'm phoning to ask you to come to the Embassy."

"The Embassy? Now? But ..."

"Please accept my apologies, but I'm appealing to you as a doctor."

"I'm listening."

"Can we pick you up in half an hour?"

"I can drive myself."

"In that case I'll be waiting for you outside."

And all the while I thought I'd forgotten. I didn't. It was huddled in the farthest corner of the heart, waiting for the right moment. At the same time the alarm came to life too, the same that sounded when I first met Ana-Maria, making me think it was wrong to go to the party. I'm not sure why I'd thought it then or now, as I was driving to the Embassy. I had no idea what worried or frightened me. Everything was so vivid in my memory as if it happened a few hours ago rather than two months ago. The call was certainly the continuation of that day, otherwise there was nothing that connected me to the Embassy.

A tall man was pacing the pavement at the Embassy gate. He was only in a suit though it was quite chilly. He put his head through the window as soon as I stopped.

"Are you the doctor?"

"I am."

"Hello. I called you."

"Shall I park here?"

"Yes, you can. The police officer will look after it." There was a police booth at the gate. "Please follow me. I'll show you the way."

We went into the hall and climbed the stairs. We passed a long half-lit passage on the first floor. He opened the last door and indicated to me to follow. The room was empty. He knocked gently on the other door. Without waiting for an answer, he opened it and let me go first. He stepped in after me. Closed the door carefully. Immediately I met Ana-Maria's eyes. She was propped up in bed, with pillows behind her back. A plaid blanket covered her legs. The Ambassador was in the armchair by the bed. A woman in a white apron was busy at the bedside table.

The Ambassador got to his feet: "I'm very sorry to have bothered you at such an hour. Thank you indeed for coming."

I refrained from looking at Ana-Maria. But I sensed her gaze. For some reason I found it hard to look in her direction.

"Please, have a seat," the Ambassador said pointing at the armchair he had just vacated. "We'll leave you. Once again, please accept my gratitude, doctor."

All three went out. For a while Ana-Maria and I stared at each other without a word, as if unconfident of our voices.

Then Ana-Maria smiled: "Do you recognize me?"

"Sure I do!"

"Hello." She stretched out her hand.

It felt like touching a pleasantly cool creature. I pushed the armchair closer. I was trying hard to conceal my overpowering agitation. I felt her pulse. She had terrible tachycardia.

"I was given buckets of heart drops," she said with a smile, "but medicine doesn't work for me. Also, you were bothered for nothing because it's a straightforward psychopathy. Who phoned you? How come they had your number? I was told to expect a doctor, but I'd never imagined it'd be you. Why have they decided I needed a psychiatrist? I'm not extremely surprised though." She showed me her bandaged wrist. "What else could they've done? Lulu stopped the bleeding pretty fast. She's incredible." She must have referred to the woman who was in the room earlier. "Anyway, it's my first time with a psychiatrist. Since you've gone to all the trouble of coming over, I'll try to be a good patient. Go on, ask your questions."

I smiled: "Frankly, I don't know what to ask."

"I like that," she said. "I dread questions. I'm a little weak, but that's all."

"Can I take your blood pressure, Ana-Maria?"

"You remember my name?" She looked away, then added, "I also remember yours. It's Levan, isn't it?"

"Thanks for not forgetting me."

"I don't want my blood pressure taken. I've never had problems with it."

She closed her eyes.

"Are you sleepy?"

"No, no! Don't go away!" she sounded anxious.

"I'm not leaving yet. If you weren't afraid of questions, I'd ask you something."

"Such as? Why I did this?" she lifted her bandaged wrist.

"Don't move it!" I scolded her with a smile.

"I'm being childish," she sounded apologetic. "I'm not sure how to behave in a situation like this. I'm bewildered. I don't recognize myself. You'd probably like to ask if I've got a family history of insanity. But you're reluctant because I'm scared of questions, right? No, there's been no insanity in the family. They all are healthy, normal, a bit too normal for my liking, and too healthy, in other words, ideal citizens. I'll make your life easier, especially since you're my guest. So what if you're a doctor and I'm your patient? That doesn't interfere with the traditional rules of hospitality. I'm talking too excitedly, aren't I?"

"No, no, go on. Thanks for helping me."

"Yes," she said, "I'm acting as your assistant. My dad is Swedish but has spent all his life in Paris. My mum's French while my grandma, the maternal one—you're not going to guess her nationality." She paused. She played with her hair, holding it in two fingers. She closed her eyes.

"Go to sleep," I told her very quietly and rose.

She opened her eyes, looking at me as if she'd never seen me before.

"No, no. Sorry," she added. "I was just thinking of my grandma. Even saw her in my mind's eye—tall and grey, dressed in black. Very upright and prim. Mother used to say I had an old guardsman for a granny. She died at ninety. Quite unexpectedly. We were dining. She folded her napkin, put it into the ring, placed the fork and knife on the plate and died. Without a word. She was Georgian. Yes, dear doctor, originally from your country. The descendant of the first wave immigrants. Her name was Nino, after your saint. When we arrived, I asked my husband to take me to Bodbe where I knew Saint Nino was buried. Incidentally, my Georgian was pretty decent when I was a child. Granny used to talk only in Georgian to me. She didn't know other languages, struggled with French. I recorded the tolling of the Bodbe Monastery bells, so every time I think of Granny, I listen to the recording. Every church bell across the world has its unique sound, different from others. And every nation tells its own story through their bells." She went quiet, then added in a whisper, "I'm tired. Please, excuse me."

"All right. Enough for now. Please calm down."

She turned her head away.

"Try to sleep now. Good night."

She said nothing but as I rose to my feet, she called me: "Levan!"

"Yes?" I sat in the armchair again.

She didn't turn her head to look at me, only whispered: "Thank you."

I found the Ambassador, his secretary, and Lulu in the other room. As I entered, the Ambassador and the secretary rose to their feet.

"Please have a seat," the Ambassador indicated a seat next to him.

We all sat down.

There was a bottle of whiskey in the middle of the table with several glasses around it.

"Would you like some whiskey?" the Ambassador asked. "We can ask Lulu to make coffee for you."

Lulu left the room at once, to get the coffee, I presumed.

"Thank you," I said. "With pleasure."

The Ambassador immediately poured me some whiskey which I drained in one swig. That minute I had desperately needed a strong drink.

"Some more?"

"No, thank you."

"Your French is very impressive." The Ambassador poured some whiskey for himself.

"I worked in Switzerland for ten years," I said.

"Oh, Switzerland, Switzerland," he said and repeated after a pause, "Switzerland."

It seemed we were trying to avoid talking about the really important issue. Anyway, personally I had no clue what to tell him. Inadvertently, as a doctor, I had witnessed something which is not discussed in families, which is evaded at all costs.

A lengthy silence followed.

Finally Lulu brought my coffee. I tasted it and complimented her on its flavor.

I broke the awkward silence: "Has she made any attempt before?" I stretched my hand towards a cigarette pack in front of the Ambassador. "May I?"

"Please do," he offered me the pack and held his lighter to my cigarette.

The Embassy Secretary and Lulu were staring at the Ambassador, who didn't rush with his reply. Instead he asked me: "Do you mean a suicide attempt?"

Reluctantly, I said: "Unfortunately, we can't call it anything else."

"No," he replied. "We've been married for three years. It came as a total surprise."

"She's extremely emotional," the Ambassador went on. "Reads a lot," suddenly, as if predicting my next question, he added hastily, "no, she doesn't watch TV. Just doesn't like it, surprising as that might be. However, one thing is really worrying—since we moved here, she spends most of her time at home. Several times I invited the wives and daughters of the diplomatic corps especially for her. A couple of times they invited her to their places, but it didn't work for her at all. In truth, she shouldn't have found it hard to get on with them, considering that she speaks several languages. She's Swedish but her upbringing and inner nature is purely French. Her mother is French, which means a lot as you might guess. I believe I've answered all your questions, even the unasked ones. If you've got more, please don't hesitate. With doctors even the diplomats are truthful," he smiled. "That's it ... Oh, nearly forgot! We don't have children but it's not the fault of either of us."

"All's fine," I said. "Her mind is clear and sharp. Any family conflict ..."

He interrupted: "Nothing of the kind."

Lulu and the secretary looked at me as if I'd mentioned something utterly unimaginable.

"Good to hear that," I said. "I just asked because, I hope you understand, it's an obligatory question in similar cases."

"I love my wife. We married for love and the feeling hasn't faded in the least in these past few years. Besides, I highly respect her."

"Love already presupposes respect," I said and added hastily, "I don't see anything alarming. And the fact that she doesn't watch TV is quite good. What about a computer? Has she got one?"

"She hates computers."

"Very good. Actually, for someone who reads a lot, the computer is less dangerous. In our case the most undesirable thing is being at home, spending time inside. At the same time, any forceful relationship can bring nil results, in fact, even be more damaging— she might start to shun all people. That's why she needs to go out in the fresh air, take long walks. There are plenty of places of interest in our city."

"Yes, she likes the city very much," the Ambassador said. "A couple of times she went to the theatre. I'm not sure if she's told you that one of her ancestors was Georgian."

"She has." I took another cigarette from the pack. I had left mine at home. The Ambassador held the lighter.

"Incidentally, she understands Georgian but can't speak it. Would you like more whiskey?"

"Yes, please, just a little. Thank you."

"Are you wondering why we called you? And at such an hour?" he asked and went on without waiting for my reply. "I came across your number among her things." He was looking at Lulu as he said it. "Here, have a look," he showed me my business card on which I had written, or rather hastily scribbled: *A psychiatrist.* "Did she ask for your phone number?"

"No, she didn't. To tell you the truth, I don't remember the context but it was at your party. Long ago, when you had that garden party. Why would I have written my profession when the name of the clinic is there, on the card, together with all phone numbers? I've got no idea how it happened."

I sounded as if I was trying to justify myself.

"Did you feel the necessity?" the Ambassador asked.

"Excuse me?" I didn't get his meaning.

He repeated his question. Of course this time I understood what he meant.

"No, can't say I did … Most probably I acted on a hunch."

I lied. I'd never ever in my life done anything like that! So what happened that evening at the garden party that made me scribble *a psychiatrist* on the card?

The Ambassador seemed to read my thoughts and calmly went on "interrogating" me. Yes, now our conversation resembled a real interrogation and I, surprisingly, felt like a culprit. Hard as I tried, I couldn't remember anything wrong or insulting from the things I might have said or done at that party which could have been regarded as offensive or unacceptable for my new acquaintance. I didn't recall breaking any unwritten ethical laws.

"So, that's what you generally add to your business card, right?"

"Yes, that's my habit," gradually I was getting annoyed, even angry. But most of all it was my almost childish vulnerability that exasperated me. I could do nothing with it, just revert to lies. At the same time, the startlingly terrifying feeling that had gripped me in the adjacent room hadn't disappeared yet, the one that stunned me not long ago. No, not me but someone else—a creature hiding in me, ready to burst out, the one that nearly inhaled, sucked in, and merged with the pale woman reclining on the cushions. "Ana-Maria!" it bellowed, moaned, and groaned the only word the creature could produce, and there was no power to keep it in check. Luckily, it had coiled back, just like a wave rolling over the sand. The momentary frenzy, that all-embracing insanity vanished as fast as it erupted and I was able to hear Ana-Maria's voice: "She used to speak Georgian to me, read Georgian fairy-tales to me." It was the voice that brought me to my senses with a jolt, as if I was hit on the head with a bat. It didn't dazzle but actually sobered me: indeed, I was primarily guilty of my life and myself and secondly I was accountable to this highly intelligent, sly and shrewd man who was more interested in something other than my diagnosis.

"And you believe she doesn't need any medicine, don't you?"

"She could take Lexotanil for a couple of days."

"Oh, Switzerland!" he seemed familiar with the pills.

"One pill twice a day, in the morning and late in the evening. Nothing else," I replied calmly, as if I hadn't gone through the unbearable ordeal just seconds ago. "And she should spend more time in the fresh air."

"My apologies," the Ambassador said, "for ruining your night." He got to his feet and we followed suit. "I'm sure it's unnecessary to remind you that . . ." he was smiling at me.

I guessed what he was about to say: "I'm a doctor. Please rest assured . . ."

Now it was his turn to interrupt me: "Thank you very much, doctor," he stretched out his hand.

The Embassy Secretary saw me to the gates. As I opened the car door, he said: "I might phone you again, with your permission."

"Please do," I replied. "And I can call here myself."

"As for the fee . . ."

"No," I stopped him. "Please, don't mention it."

When I got home, I didn't even take off my coat. I just sat on the steps for a while, strangely agitated . . .

I phoned the Embassy the next day. The phone was answered by a woman. Probably Lulu.

"Embassy speaking!"

"Can I speak to Ana-Maria?"

"Who is this, please?"

I presented myself.

"Hello, doctor," she said in an icy voice, "Ana-Maria is sleeping."

"How is she?"

"Better, thank you."

"Can you please tell her I phoned?"

"I will. Thank you, doctor," she said and hung up.

Three days passed. I walked around delirious. I went about my usual duties at the clinic and the institute mechanically. Even when

I talked to others, I could hear my voice from afar, as if someone else was echoing me, just like it sometimes happens on the phone.

"You need a woman, buddy," my colleague told me when we were drinking beer in our usual diner. "What's wrong with our girls—Mzia, Viola, or Albina? Grab any of them, take them places. Do you think they'll mind? No. In fact, they'll be ecstatic!"

"Leave me alone," I told him. "I don't want to hear about women at the moment."

Three days later I called the Embassy again. A man answered the phone. When I said who I was, he suddenly sounded animated: "Oh, we've met. I'm the Secretary. I was about to phone you at the Ambassador's request. We wanted to ask for a favor, if it's not too much trouble and it won't interfere with your other personal plans."

My heart was thumping madly: "I'm at your disposal," I said. "I'd be happy to help if I can."

"It's sheer telepathy. Amazing, isn't it? I was about to call you and suddenly you phone me." The Secretary sounded genuinely amused at the coincidence or else he was playing for time.

"It happens," I said, "quite often, actually."

"I'm afraid I can't agree," he speedily retorted. "However, you might be right, but for me it's the first time." His voice changed to a more official register. "And how are you?"

"Thanks," I said. "I'm fine."

"We are really sorry about the other night. We would like to apologize once more for bothering you."

"That's okay," I replied. "It's not altogether unusual for me. I'm a doctor, remember?"

"In fact, I was going to phone you with a medical favor."

"Yes?"

"If on Sunday, that's the day after tomorrow, you are free, unburdened with other urgent cases or scheduled meetings ..."

"What about Sunday?"

"Yes, as I was saying," he seemed irritated by my interruption, "Maybe you could call on Ana-Maria on Sunday? We'd like her, of course if you have nothing against it, to go for a walk with you.

Anywhere, provided she breathes the fresh air as you prescribed. It's going to be her first stroll for a very long time, as you can guess ..."

I couldn't control my voice. His worried voice shook me out of the trance: "Hello! Hello! Hello!"

"I'm still here," I finally got the words out.

"I thought we were disconnected."

"I'll be there on Sunday."

"That's wonderful," he exclaimed.

"I've got nothing planned for Sunday."

"So, we've agreed, right?"

"What time can I call on her?"

"Around midday. Can you?"

"Fine. I'll be there at noon."

"Thank you very much. Good-bye then."

"Good-bye."

We ended our weird conversation. Weird because I expected anything except such a proposition, a precious gift sent from the heavens ...

The Moscow clinic was different from the one in Tbilisi only in its cleanliness, otherwise it was the same. However, here we were taken for interrogation at night. We would be driven somewhere and I was unable to find out the name of the place where we were taken into separate rooms for questioning. I always got a different investigator. The rooms were clones of one another: pictures of Felix Dzerzhinsky, a water carafe, a glass, a flower pot on the window sill, metal bars on the windows, and a towel hanging from the nail on the inside of the door. They made me tell my story over and over again, but this time the interrogation was done through an interpreter because I had lied about my Russian, saying it was so bad they wouldn't understand anything. Strangely enough, they brought an Armenian from Tbilisi to do the job. He wore a grey worsted wool suit and a pair of grey squeaky shoes. He translated really well. As soon as there was a break, he praised Tbilisi, in Russian of course. He was forbidden to speak Georgian to me. My narrative in his translation was recorded on several occasions, then the versions were compared to each other to find discrepancies.

Earlier, before I was transferred to Moscow, I was woken up at the crack of dawn, put into a helicopter and flown to Abastumani. I was taken to the cave. There were more soldiers there. Must have discovered the cave quite recently. I was asked to tell my story again. I did. In full detail, without missing a single thing. Including the grave. Of course I didn't mention the ranger. I said I'd found him already dead and buried him. The whole area was dug up and they did more digging while I was there. They found nothing, neither the grave nor the dead. I guess Carlo, the ranger, had taken care of them. I did feel hurt because I thought the rascal didn't trust me. Finally I was taken into the cave.

"Did you screw here?" one of the KGB officers asked me.

"Yes," I replied calmly.

"Valiko!" the other officer scolded the first one.

"She's lying. All of it is a cock and bull story!" Valiko sounded angry.

"She's not lying. She's just mad," his comrade reassured him. "These lunatics are what they are because they can't lie."

"I'm not mad," I said.

"Very good," he replied. "What can be better?"

I spent ten years in the Moscow clinic. There's plenty written about the institution. I don't suppose I can add anything new to it. I'd just like to tell a rather romantic story that happened to me, more precisely actually, I was witness to it. The story had a predictably banal ending.

Needless to say, men and women were kept in separate wards, even separate buildings. But we used to meet quite often. It was the time when the Soviet psychiatric clinics were full of the so-called dissidents, in other words, not just normal, but extremely sharp and intelligent people. You could come across amazingly interesting individuals as well as the usual scum. Some of them were KGB stool pigeons. We were looked after by an army of military women masquerading as our nurses.

There was a young man among the patient-inmates: skinny, spectacled, a poet and a philosopher, Lev Shestov's descendant. He had a permanent cold, complete with a running nose and a crumpled wet handkerchief in his hand. Other dissidents treated him with marked reverence, called him Yuri Leonidovich, using his patronymic name out of respect. He was known for his exceptional loyalty to the cause, having gained the authority in the free-thinking circles for courageously defending justice. At the end of every month the KGB would raid Yuri Leonidovich's ward, diligently frisking his possessions. They must have known pretty well in advance what to look for and where exactly—the manuscripts! I still believe it was an unofficial agreement between the predator and the prey. They said the KGB were smuggling his works abroad, selling them profitably, exactly as they did with Solzhenitsyn or Pasternak's *Doctor Zhivago*. Incidentally, there were books in the clinic library, unimaginable as it is for a clinic like that to have a library at all, that you couldn't find in any bookshop because they were forbidden by state censorship. In this respect the dissidents had ideal working conditions. Simultaneously, the KGB demanded more and more oppositional work from them. Understandably, it wasn't discussed openly.

Yuri Leonidovich and I used to see each other during our daily walks. Frankly speaking, I found his company extremely pleasing, probably thanks to his reverential attitude towards me. Actually I have a lot of self-respect, which I don't see as a flaw for a woman. When alone, I often thought of the young man whose habit was to rub his hands. The nineteenth century seemed to talk to me through him, or rather the Russian literature of that period, being unique and interesting for its amazing women and the attitude towards them. Admittedly, I like the nineteenth century for its humane face and think mankind should have stayed there if it wished to be saved. Young Yuri seemed to be completely ignorant of everyday life as one can only learn about by actually living it. But I had the impression he was talking to a woman for the first time. He wasn't aware of the simplest things that even the most primitive bumpkin would revert to if he wanted to win a woman. Another thing he didn't know was that by quoting appropriate authors, their fully-internalized phrases, he succeeded in boosting a woman's — in this case, my — craving for life. Inadvertently, it certainly turned him into a highly attractive person. Men learned to speak beautifully only to attract females. Women are well aware of that fact and need to hear those beautiful words as proof of their femininity. I seem to hear all my sisters' pleas from nuptial beds, brothel windows, bushes, and dark alleys: "Tell me, please tell me! Say it, you fool!" Women need those words that men see as utterly nonsensical. In exactly the same way, the words the blushing Yuri was saying to me there and then were absolutely essential to me. In fact, he was looking somewhere above my head, well into the space, just like an anchor looks at a teleprompt propped up somewhere beyond the camera. He was the only man in my life who was content if I just listened to him. He demanded nothing else. The fool.

My husband, who I'd treated dreadfully, was a cynic, mocking me and himself which, I guess, brought about his end. In truth, he had been committing suicide every single day before actually taking down the gun, putting it under his chin and, like his father, pulling the trigger with the bare big toe. I was reminded of the poet because one fine day he asked me to marry him! I laughed, wondering about the reasons why he was ready to sacrifice himself. I told him he was absolutely sane and I didn't see why he needed a mad wife. Even if I agreed, I reasoned with him, one day he'd be set free because Mr Suslov, that ice phallus, would melt sooner or later. (Instead of a phallus, of course I used another word, more emphatic and more commonly used in our environment.) Did he want to end up with another disaster on his hands? Besides, I'd been a poet's wife once and the end was pretty tragic, I said. What you need, my boy, doesn't necessarily require marriage, I added. Then I told him the story of what brought me to the psychiatric clinic. He didn't know anything about me. I saw he was scared. He immediately believed I was insane. After that he avoided me, averting his gaze when we bumped into each other during our walks. Curiously, I had accepted my insanity. Accepted and calmed down. Everything fell into place …

"I'm not sure why I'm telling you all this and in such detail. I think that somehow every word bears a very special meaning and that if I omit even one, which quite probably I will anyway, I won't make myself understood. You must be thinking I'm really insane, aren't you?"

"No, that's not what I think," Levan smiled.

"But what about my prattle? How can one talk for so long? Thank you for not stopping me. I know I've taken a lot of your time."

"Didn't you say the world was full of time?"

"You remember that, don't you? Nobody seems to have enough time these days mainly because we don't know its true value. We can't really measure time in hours, can we? Does it measure with clocks and calendars? Can it reflect the time I spent in the clinic? Was it the ordinary ten years? I think it should be called something else, but, sadly, I don't know any other word to apply to it. Neither does anyone else. How can one define how long it takes a gliding leaf to die? For us it might be a minute, but what about the leaf itself? It's only us, people, who measure time, and we always do it as it suits us. But have we got the right? Are you going to say I'm not suffering from barylalia?"

"Your speech is very fluent."

"My husband used to say the same. The cynic."

"Please trust me."

"Are you interested in what I'm telling you?"

"Sure I am!"

"Amazing!"

"What is amazing?"

"That you find it interesting."

"What makes you say so?"

"I'm not sure . . ."

She lit a cigarette. Was quiet for some time. Levan waited patiently for Nunu to continue.

"Can I have some water?"

"Yes, of course. Just a second."

He brought her some water.

"Thanks," the woman said. She drank a little. "My mouth gets dry," she smiled, "from so much talk. At the end of the Perestroika period I was transferred back to Tbilisi, to the clinic of course. The same one I was moved to from your clinic. Nothing had changed there since my times. The same patients, the same doctors, nurses, the same wardens and janitors—everything was the same! Even worse—once, I opened the wrong door and saw a couple of wardens over poor Bella who was lying on the table with her skirt up to her chin. She was eating maize as usual. It appeared to be the same one. I quickly closed the door. Leaned against it. A strange feeling of peacefulness filled me, something I'd never experienced before. Something which is typical for a traditionally conventional lifestyle. Didn't I say that time doesn't move, or rather that it exists as a completely different dimension?

Tbilisi was in turmoil at the time. The city rumbled, in a muffled and dangerous way. And the rumbling reached us too. But like a wave over the sand, it went through the sieve of cretinism, hunger, and filth. We were hungry. On Sundays my mum, more precisely her lover—she changed husbands, but not her lover—would bring food in a basket covered with a snow-white cloth. The basket would be empty in a matter of seconds. I rarely got any of the food as I was reluctant to be part of the scuffle around it. Unlike Moscow, there was only one dissident here, or rather a former dissident. At the time of his admission he must have been absolutely sane, but gone nuts in the clinic. He used to take me away from the others, get his dick out, and ask in a whisper: 'Ma'am, do you like my capital I?' And all the while his eyes would dart as if he were an illegal dealer in stolen goods. I always laughed out loud. And he'd walk away making those funny cackling noises. Must have liked his own joke. But was it a joke? There was another one, called King Lear probably because he was looking for his land. Used to yell at everyone: 'What have you done to my country, you bitches!' He would search for his lost land under the beds, behind cupboards, inside people's bags. When finished with his futile search, he'd turn his palms up and shout: 'I'm hungry, people! Can you hear me? I'm hungry!'

On sunny days I used to stay in the garden, greedily catching warm sunshine with my eyes shut keeping my hands under my armpits. I could stand like that for hours. Not having hot water was most upsetting. A woman shouldn't go insane, especially in places where there are such clinics. I hope you've guessed I've been avoiding certain details, as you are perfectly aware of the conditions in our hospitals. That's why I won't bother you with the petty facts which you know even better than I do. Besides it's not necessary. They say people get used to anything. Even to insanity, if such a thing can be imagined. A person can live or exist like a lunatic though can be quite normal and it's precisely that insane life or existence that allows one to cope and be strong. It seems that coping and adapting make a human life, but how can they be measured?

We mourned the tragic events of the 9th of April in our own

way. We howled like animals for two days and nights. That's how time passed for us, those left out of Time. My parents used to visit me, separately of course as they had been divorced for quite some time. Mother was invariably accompanied by her lover, an attractive graying man. I knew he was a swimming instructor and a pretty popular masseur. They used to bring clothes and plenty of food which, as I already said, I immediately distributed among other patients. My parents had never asked me why I ended up in the clinic, what had happened, what I had done to deserve being in an asylum. They believed the official statement—their daughter was insane. Nothing doing. Such things happen. In general, my parents tended not to question whatever the government chose to say, especially things broadcast on TV.

One day, quite unexpectedly, we were given such a lot of food and drink at the clinic that the patients not only ate what they could but seriously overate. They howled, sang, cried, rolled in their own vomit, but still ate and drank. Just like the ancient Romans, someone joked. Then, all of a sudden, everyone felt drowsy. Soon the whole clinic was sleeping as if doped. We slept for several hours before being unceremoniously woken up with loud: Get up! Fast! Put your best clothes on! Double quick! As if we had the clothes we could choose from. We were yelled at by completely unknown people, rushed to the gates where they already had trucks waiting for us. They were clearly KGB officers. I always recognize their voices and their manner of speaking. Even today, here and there, I keep hearing that peculiar speech in quite unexpected places.

'Shall we take the idiots too?' one of them asked.

'Leave them behind,' he was told. 'Only the mad ones.'

'Okay, nitwits, into the trucks! Move, move, double quick! You're being taken on an outing. Move! Or do you prefer a cold shower? Shall I get a hose? Move, double quick!' We were put in the trucks with tarpaulin tops. When we got to Dzneladze Street, we were pushed from the trucks. 'Quick! Stand together, in a row!' a tall man shouted at us. We did as we were told. The air was strangely unclear, pale and faded. The lampposts gave out a yellow light that painted all faces yellow. Not far from us there was a children's group with banners. They were oddly quiet. An indistinct din reached us from Rustaveli Avenue, the street above.

'Who have you brought?' someone yelled. 'Where did you find these scarecrows?'

I immediately recognized the voice. He was another KGB man. I had been talking to them much too often, in Tbilisi as well as in Moscow. A KGB agent has no nationality. It's a special breed of people, worked on like, say, a Doberman pinscher.

'Didn't you say to bring the lunatics?' one of our accompanying officers reacted.

'Fucking fool,' his superior got furious. 'How can I trust them to shout what's needed?'

I guessed at once we were brought to disrupt the rally.

'And so I brought the lunatics,' our officer argued.

'Are you fucking nuts? Think we're short of loonies?' Suddenly he turned to me, 'You, for instance, do you know what you're supposed to shout?'

'Of course, you fucking fool,' I replied calmly, 'we know very well.'

'Call her loony if you wish!' someone laughed.

'I asked if you know what to shout,' the senior officer came nearer.

'Long live freedom!' I shouted while others joined me: 'We're hungry! Hungry! Hungry!'

'To hell with you,' the senior said and walked away.

The lunatics, meaning us, were standing aloof, keeping to ourselves. We thumped our feet, huffed at our hands. It was too cold. No doctor had accompanied us because the whole medical staff of our clinic had been going to the rallies over the past couple of days. We patiently waited for new orders.

Someone new came running: 'Ma'am, are you a doctor?'

He either singled me out because of my height or my clothes because I was dressed much better than the others.

'You can take your patients back. The truck is waiting at the end of the street.'

'I need a whistle,' I said. For some reason I felt like joking. Possibly because he mistook me for a doctor. But he bought it and called out to the policeman: 'Come here, lad!'

'Yes, sir!' the policeman rushed to us.

'Give this lady here your whistle!'

'How can I, chief?' the policeman sounded worried. 'It gives me my daily bread.'

'I said, give it!' the KGB officer raised his voice.

Blowing into my new whistle, I headed home. No one stopped me. I walked and whistled. When I came near my house, I met Mother. She was walking the dog.

'Nunu?' she was so shocked to see me, she couldn't move.

I blew my whistle.

'What are you doing here?'

Instead of answering her I blew the whistle again.

'Why aren't you there?' she sounded genuinely worried.

I walked past her, without a word. That's how I achieved independence several months earlier than Georgia.

I had the keys to my flat. I stretched across the bed without taking off my clothes. The next morning I woke up quite early. Mother came over later. I was sitting at the mirror, combing my hair. More precisely, I held my hair in a fist at the back and was examining my reflection. Mother made me open my fist, took the comb and began to brush my hair, just like in my childhood. She was reciting a near forgotten nursery rhyme. I grabbed her hand and said, more to myself than to Mother, that I was old …

In the beginning I seldom left home. And nobody visited me from the clinic. After a while a fire destroyed the local KGB office, apparently burning my dossier among other documents. I lived alone. Mother moved in with her new husband, Dad had long ago gone to live with his new wife. At first I found it hard to communicate with friends and acquaintances alike, but soon I discovered there wasn't much difference between 'here' and 'there', the place where I had been locked up for so long. However, I also found out that living with the so-called 'normal' people was more difficult than with the 'abnormal' ones. On the other hand, perhaps I had lost the knack.

Ten years is no joke, especially if measured in traditional units. My most significant discovery, though, was that normality was an extremely conventional notion. A Frenchman said once, 'If you want to be seen as normal, you need to be a thoroughbred rascal.' I suppose no clinic uses the amount of psychotropic medicine a single so-called normal person can consume in a day. I was absolutely shocked to see Mother's medical cabinet—I had never seen so many pills, in either the Tbilisi or the Moscow clinic!

Mother took care of the dog. It was her main job, though she also gave lectures at the university. The tiny jealous creature with long ears and long hair hated me. He barked at me all the time, non-stop. Neither did Mother's 'Kote, stop it, Kote!' help. She loved it so much that she named it after her first husband, that's my dad. In fact, it was her lover who now looked after me. His responsibility now included caring for two women—Mother and me. His name was Gela. He had nobody in the whole world except us. He was exceptionally honest and attentive. Used to go to the market and prepare meals. You should have seen him in the kitchen, with rolled sleeves, in Mother's pink apron. Once I told him it was very becoming. He didn't respond. In general, he didn't talk much. In the evenings he would bid us goodbye as we, already fed, curled up in front of our TVs. He did it separately because Mother lived one floor above me, in her new husband's flat. My new stepfather rarely came down from Tskneti, the hilly suburb.

Gela lived on his own, all alone. Though we were a pair who constantly required looking after, it still seemed he needed us more than we needed him. Born to be a family man, loving and caring, he had none due to life's strange whims. But what would you expect after meeting Mother? She insisted that Gela give me massages too. He had amazingly nimble fingers. Sinking into a relaxing drowsiness, I used to lie with closed eyes, wondering about his limitless patience and calm. I used to step naked into the bathroom which he warmed for me, lie in the bath filled with the water which he heated for me, then he would pour warm water over me from a white jug, wrap me in a big fluffy towel and dry me as if I were a baby. Doesn't your man have a hard-on anymore? I once asked Mother. Instead of replying, she just giggled. However, at one point he gave in. That day as I stepped out of the bath, we stood very close to each other. Of course unintentionally, he pressed his face to my breasts. I was a bit taller than him. He took my nipple and, with his eyes closed, sucked at it as if were a sweet. It didn't last long and it was the farthest we went that time. For several years all was as usual — he would massage me, pour warm water over me to rinse the soap off, wrap me up, and dry me off.

My stepfather refused to come down from Tskneti even when Mum was dying. He was guarding his house, fearing squatters could take over if he left it unattended. Gela and I stayed by Mother's deathbed. She took our hands, crossed them, as if leaving me in his care. Now Gela only looks after me. Nothing much has changed for him except that he's sharing the bed with his former lover's daughter. What had to happen actually did happen, as it was the most natural thing between a man and a woman. In this respect, I've always wanted normal relationships, but more often than not I was a victim of some kind of pathology. And I don't mean those moments when the heavens came into me.

In the evenings Gela and I take little Kote for walks. He doesn't bark at me anymore. Even dogs reconcile with their fate. Smoking a cigarette, big Kote — I mean Dad — sometimes waves to us from his balcony. Apparently, he isn't allowed to smoke inside.

Gela doesn't stay with me at night. He usually goes to his own place in Sololaki. He's changed his car. Instead of the old Moskvich, now he's got a second-hand Opel, a well-used one. German cars, it seems, never get old. Nowadays when everything is measured by its prestige value, or rather, it is nothing if it's unprestigious, the popular, prestigious masseur is earning quite well. Women like him but Gela is surprisingly loyal, which annoys me in a way, because it burdens me with unwanted responsibility. But I think you already know I can't stand duties and responsibilities. That's how I've lived for several years. I've been working in one of the publishing houses as an editor of school books ..."

7

Exactly at noon I was standing at the Embassy gates. Ana-Maria appeared almost immediately through the main door of the building. She wasn't accompanied but I was absolutely sure many pairs of eyes watched us from all windows. She was wearing a gray French tweed coat with the collar lifted up and a long yellow scarf. Before I got there I was extremely nervous but as soon as I saw her, I calmed down surprisingly quickly. I got out of my car, greeted her by putting two fingers to my forehead. She smiled:

"Hello, Levan."

"Hello, Ana-Maria."

She had low-heeled shoes on but was still slightly taller than me. I opened the passenger door for her.

"Thanks," she got in.

"Where to?"

"Doesn't really matter," she replied. "The main thing is to be in the fresh air, as you prescribed. I was advised to try Turtle Lake, what do you think? I've discovered that Lulu jogs around the lake every morning."

That meant we were going to Turtle Lake. She was given the directions, and we were supposed to follow them.

The lake looked utterly abandoned. The mud-colored water stood still, as if smoothed with a hand. A boat without oars was tied to the wooden pier. The slopes of the hill around the lake were covered in hoar-frost. A weary, weak November sun spread thinly over the ground like a glittery translucent fabric. There was no one around except us and a driver changing the tire of his Niva at the restaurant door.

"There are more people here in the mornings, like Lulu," I told Ana-Maria. "Mainly well-off people, I mean politicians, worried about their health."

We walked and talked, slowly, along the bank, circling the lake twice.

"It looks like a turtle," Ana-Maria smiled. "That's probably why it's called Turtle Lake."

"Are you cold?" I asked.

"A little," she said, "but if you're not tired, can we walk a little longer? I haven't walked for ages."

For a while we went on without talking. Then she stopped, turned to me and said: "I'd like you to know that I'm not insane, but I do need a psychiatrist. I feel the need but can't explain why. Possibly because even now, as I look at this miserable lake, I seem to be dreaming of it. In my dream it's somewhere else, in the bright sunshine, glistening like a huge shop window. There are crowds everywhere and they don't look like either the Georgians or those from my country. They are absolutely different, but quite familiar and dear to me. I've never thought of people in this way. This isn't the first time I've dreamt it. It usually comes back slightly altered every time. The landscapes of this dream are likewise familiar and dear to me, but are somewhat mysterious at the same time. The dream recurs and not necessarily only when I sleep. It jolts me out of reality at any time, just like now, when I'm wide awake. I usually feel sad, my heart heavy as I miss everything I imagine—the lake, hills, the bottomless sky, though I can be quite certain I've never seen them in reality. An inexplicable force attracts me to them, drawing me like a magnet, and I feel so helpless, so helpless!" she suddenly exclaimed, clinging to my arm with both hands. "Don't let go!" She pressed to me. I embraced her. She smiled, "I'm joking. You can let me go." She walked away and I followed her. After a while she turned to me again: "That's why I need a psychiatrist. Incidentally, I haven't told anyone else about it. Except, long ago, I told something similar to my husband. What's the psychiatric term for the disease?"

"Is it a disease? I can't say because I don't know what it is."

"Oh, I know," she said. "In psychiatry it's known as *anxietas precordialis*, which means fatal melancholy in plain language."

"How do you know?" I asked.

"Read about it in the psychiatric encyclopedia. A friend died of it recently."

"You haven't mentioned that before." I lit a cigarette.

"You never asked. Actually, I noticed you haven't even asked what happened."

"Can I remind you that you warned me you didn't like questions?"

"But you still guessed everything, didn't you?"

"I didn't, except those things which were obvious."

"Such as?"

"That you aren't ill. Generally, it's always better if you give the doctor all the details of your condition."

"I'll tell you something, but promise you won't be angry. Please say you won't be angry!"

"You've got my word."

"Funnily enough, I don't see you as a doctor though I know you're a good one."

Although her words were significant and pleasantly flattering, I pretended I didn't get their true meaning. Or even if I did, I didn't ascribe much importance to them.

I asked: "How long have you had them?"

"What? I don't understand the question."

"Those visions."

"Oh, as long as I remember myself. But lately they occur more often and are much more vivid. In other words, I'm in deep water," she laughed. "Very deep." Her expression changed. Even her voice cracked and she coughed. "Feel the chill? But I'm fine. I breathe freely and deeply."

We stopped at the restaurant. The Niva was gone.

"Don't tell me you aren't peckish," I asked with a smile.

"Famished! What's more, I haven't had anything to eat for three days. I just couldn't! They begged me to have something but I could only face juice. Orange juice."

The restaurant was empty. It was quite warm in the small hall. The glass walls were so beady you couldn't see beyond. As soon as we sat down, a waiter came to our table with a menu.

"No, thanks," I said. "Can you suggest something yourself?"

"I'd like roast beef and a glass of red wine," Ana-Maria said. "Nothing else."

"We've got Kotekhi," the waiter said. "You'll like it."

"It's very good wine, if you trust me," I told her. "From Kakheti, eastern Georgia, very traditional."

"I'm pretty good at wines," Ana-Maria laughed. "All diplomatic receptions, functions, and parties are in fact wine-tasting sessions. Wine and smiles."

After swallowing the first gulp, she said: "It's really great. That's the kind of wine I like!"

"Apart from everything else, your mother is French and your grandma Georgian. You can't go wrong, especially with Georgian wines," I smiled.

A gypsy girl of about fourteen or fifteen came into the restaurant. She looked frozen, rubbing her blue hands.

"So nice in here!" she exclaimed. "Can I have some lemonade?"

"Sure," I said.

The waiter came running towards the girl.

"How many times have I warned you not to come here? Get out, now!"

The girl turned to us: "Please, don't let him drive me out! I'll tell your fortune for you. For the beautiful lady." From her pocket she drew a pack of cards, which looked as if they had been soaked in water before being frozen. "Please, please!"

I drew up a chair for her at our table:

"Have a seat."

"Thanks." She sat down, putting the cards before her. "My name's Era. Everyone knows me. I'm a good fortune-teller."

She used a wild mixture of Georgian and Russian. Ana-Maria looked at her with a smile.

"She says she can tell your fortune," I told Ana-Maria. "Would you like her to?"

"Very much!" Ana-Maria pressed her hands to her chest. "Very much!"

"Okay, you can tell the lady's fortune," I turned to the girl. "Let's see how good you are."

"First let me drink my lemonade and give me a five-lari note. No fortune-telling without it."

I gave her the money. She hastily hid it in her bosom.

"And the lemonade?" she asked.

I beckoned the waiter who brought her lemonade, opened the bottle, and poured the drink in a glass.

"He's a human," Era said about the waiter. "I thought he was a cop." She turned one card, then another. Her gaze never left Ana-Maria's face. Then she returned both cards into the pack and said:

"No, I can't!"

"What?" I asked. "What is it?"

"I'm scared of this beautiful woman."

"Scared?" I looked at Ana-Maria, who was listening to us, leaning across the table.

"What does the little Sybil say?" she asked me without taking her eyes off the gypsy girl.

"She said she was scared."

"Of what?"

"Not of what but of whom … Of the beautiful woman."

"Scared of me?"

"That's what she said."

Ana-Maria's face changed expression. She took a cigarette from the pack.

"Can I have one?" Era made a pleading gesture by pulling at her neck.

"What did she say?" Ana-Maria asked me. "I don't seem to understand a single Georgian word."

"It's not Georgian. It's gibberish," I said with a smile. "She asks for a cigarette."

Ana-Maria pushed a pack of Camel to the girl. She took several and said: "I'm still scared."

"Why?" I asked and added, "She's a very nice lady."

"Are you going to tell me what's it's all about?" Ana-Maria was interested.

"I said her fears were groundless as you are a very, very, very nice lady."

Era poured herself some more lemonade, drank it, and belched. She tapped her lip with the back of her hand. She rose to her feet, took a pack of Marlboro from her back pocket and added the new cigarettes to the ones inside: "Thanks a lot."

"Are you still here?" the waiter spotted her.

"I'm off! Adios!" our little fortune-teller jingled and disappeared.

"A nice girl," Ana-Maria said after some time. "Frankly speaking, sometimes I fear myself. She said a strange thing. It's several months since I've started to notice it myself."

"Are you scared of yourself?"

"Yes, scared and alienated. I don't recognize myself. I suppose it's the same." She was quiet for quite a while. Neither of us uttered a word. She was deep in thought. Far away.

Then I asked: "You mentioned *anxietas precordialis* ..."

"What?" she was brought back from her reverie. "Yes, here," she put her hand over her heart. "It hurts awfully. I haven't told anybody. I don't mean the pain. It started only a week ago, quite unexpectedly. I felt, or sensed, I'm not sure how to put it—I guessed and felt that something terrible had happened. Somehow, I'd like to tell you about it, possibly because I wish to unburden myself. But it's not going to be a confession, don't be afraid. What's more, I don't expect your understanding. I just want you to listen."

"Please, don't worry," I said. "I'm eager to listen."

"Yes, I'm a little nervous. I'll try to calm down. We met in the subway. I don't remember where I was coming from but we did have enough time to realize we were attracted to each other. When we came out into the street, we sat in the nearest bistro to have some coffee. In truth, we didn't want to part. He actually said he didn't want to go anywhere. He was a teacher in one of the small villages near Paris, teaching history to kids. He was two years older than me. There, in the bistro, we agreed that every Monday I'd go to his village on my bike. He used to wait for me in the school yard together with his students. Then he would lead me to his classroom.

After two visits the kids got used to me. I sat at the back, sideways as the desk was too small and I had no legroom. He would talk excitedly, thrilled that I was there, listening to him. Like me, he had a double name: Jean Paul. He seemed to be ecstatic when teaching about Hannibal, Pompey, Sulla ... As if he were reciting a poem ... The class, including myself, was forgetting to breathe. During one of his lessons he came over to me, took the helmet I had in my lap, donned it, raised his arm like a Roman warrior and exclaimed: 'Numerous victories cannot possibly gain us as much success as we can lose by a single defeat!'

"That day we crossed our Rubicon. As soon as he suggested I visit his place with a quivering voice, I immediately agreed. He sat behind me on my bike and we headed for his house. The kids chased us with loud cheers. He was renting a loft in one of the houses ... Then we lay in the bed, eating pâté de foie gras and drinking red wine bought from the local shop. Jean Paul had pried the pâté tin open with a knife. We used the same knife to spread the pâté on bread, chasing every bite with the red wine. Taking turns to drink straight from the bottle, we finished a whole liter. I've never enjoyed any food so much in my life," she put her hand on mine and added, "excluding today's meal. Of course I'm grateful for the treat, but that one was very special. I can't lie to you." She was quiet for quite some time, then lit a cigarette. "It's all my fault."

I didn't ask what was her fault because I felt she would explain herself. Although, she clearly found it hard to talk.

"One fine day he turned up just like that, without any notice," she went on quietly. "He rang the doorbell. Mother opened the door and called me: Ana-Maria, a visitor to see you! I peeped from my room. Oh God, Jean Paul! He had a bunch of wild flowers in his hand. I had to nearly force him into the living room. He was utterly embarrassed. Mother, it's my friend, Jean Paul. Nice to meet you, Mother said. He was wearing a dark suit stinking of moth balls. I believe he'd rented it. No tie. His hair was too long, lost behind the collar. You look as though you're about to propose, Mother said when she brought a vase with water from the kitchen to put the

flowers in. I was shocked at Mother's insensitive remark, or rather
her cruelty. But I also guessed she was not so much worried by Jean
Paul's helpless look but more scared of it. Madam, he said, it's my
birthday today. I hugged him from behind and sobbed into his back
as if it was the day of his death instead of his birthday. The most important thing happened afterwards. I can't elucidate it due to its il-
logical, bizarre, and inexplicable nature because it was alarmingly
strange to me and unbearable as a result. At the time it presented
the only possible way out of the overpowering giddiness of my bliss
which, in my understanding, lay through sacrificing Jean Paul. I still
don't know why I thought so, what impelled me to arrive at such a
conclusion. Very likely it was his moth ball suit! Don't laugh!"

"I won't," I replied. "I don't see anything funny."

"You've got an amazing talent for listening."

"It's my job."

"No one is able to conceive of it. Neither can you. Please don't
be offended." Then she glanced at me because she had been looking
away until now. "No one," she repeated. "For some bizarre reason I
want to tell everything exactly as it happened, as I felt at the time,
as I suffered." She was quiet, then added, "As my soul pained." She
lit another cigarette. "I utterly hate the phrase but can't think of a
better one. I stopped seeing Jean Paul. I accepted the first marriage
proposal I was offered. We went to Algeria first and then came here,
to Georgia. Mother was very happy to hear about this posting. She
was here the year I was born, in 1980. A group of tourists attending
the Moscow Olympic Games was brought to Tbilisi for a couple of
days. Being half Georgian, Mother was always intrigued with the
country. Jean Paul didn't know about my marriage. Mother told
me about his daily phone calls. She used to do this by saying: 'He
called.' It was said in a way that left no doubt who she meant. That's
how it went on for almost three years. But he stopped calling last
month and suddenly, several days ago ..."

She stopped. Took a sip of her wine.

"Maybe you'd like to stop?" I asked.

As if she hadn't heard my words, she went on: "The strangest thing is that I felt, and I'm not exaggerating, I felt with my whole body what Mother later told me on the phone: he died in the airport departure lounge. Nobody knew where he was going to fly. He didn't even have a ticket. An excruciating pain squeezed my heart and I took a razor only to stop the unbearable pain. The worst thing, though, was that I felt I didn't love him anymore. But still, I caused his death. I was his *anxietas precordialis* ..."

When she was getting out of the car at the Embassy, she said: "I won't be seeing you again. At least I'll try not to."

I only managed to ask her: "Can I phone to ask about you?"

"I can't forbid you to do so. Thank you very much. I'll never forget this day."

A week went by, then another. I called several times but she never answered the phone. Instead, it was the invariably composed Lulu who told me that Ana-Maria was much better, thank you, doctor, and that she'd inform her that I asked after her.

Everything seemed to go back to normal. Actually not, because after the recent, extremely unusual emotional turmoil which guarded my head and heart, I found myself leading a rather uninspiring, mundane life, very much typical for my numerous colleagues and friends: home, clinic, home, occasional visit to or from a friend, a chance meeting or a one-off date. The only new thing, rather alarming I thought at the time, was that I started to drink more. But I couldn't fight it. The most disturbing thing was that it didn't matter what the drink was. I truly worried because I had found "the most reliable and well-trodden road to the truth," as one of my friends said. I used to get home quite late and immediately switch on the TV. I'd sit in an armchair in front of it, still in my coat. I was too lazy to change clothes. And I'd doze off. At midnight I'd be woken up by the TV, jolted out of my dream. What? Where am I? I'd sit up, my heart pounding, limbs trembling. Then I changed out of my work clothes, or rather changed for bed. I used to take a book and though I was reading my favorite poems, my mind was elsewhere— in the restaurant with Ana-Maria. And then I wrestled with my memory. I wanted to hide from it, trying to recall other memories to overshadow the painful one. I strived to bring forth thousands of other things rather than concentrate on the most acute recollection. And yet, out of the bottomless pit called memory—possibly to make it sound more appealing—filled with broken or shattered objects, with faceless masks of familiar and unfamiliar people, the name Ana-Maria would surge up, erupting from the depths, surfacing like a whale from the ocean deep. The oddity didn't lie in the fact that I couldn't control myself, that my self-preservation instinct struggled to forget the name in order to save me. The strangest turn was that instead of Ana-Maria (actually, I couldn't recall her face at all!), I pictured a tiny boat without oars tied to the wooden pier at Turtle Lake. The image haunted me like a nightmare, and I recoiled from it because my heart burned unbearably. The ache was more dangerous than the physical one as it didn't kill me but made my existence agonizingly painful.

It must have been the result of my mood at the time which impelled me write in my diary: *I'd like to hold you in my fist, knead like clay and sculpt you anew ... The same you!* It sounded strange. As if someone else had written it and was drunk too. In truth, whether written by me or someone else, the wish looked like a drunken man's drivel. No way could it continue like that! I even toyed with the idea of moving to Batumi where I was offered a better job and a higher salary. But I was burdened with certain responsibilities in Tbilisi though the innovative reforms made my life-long career seem a bit vague. As if someone somewhere didn't want me to do my job well. Instead of thinking about my patients, now I was forced to worry about not turning into one of them myself. I slammed the diary shut as if a vicious beast growled at me from the pages. I won't drink from this moment! Not a drop of alcohol! Why have I been drinking anyway? Was I hiding from someone or simply from myself? No way, my dear, you're going to hide from yourself. But what do I do? What do I do now? I roamed the house. Up and down the stairs. Opening cupboard doors and drawers as if searching my own place without knowing what I was looking for. I came across Ia's things nearly everywhere. The walk-in wardrobe was still full of her clothes! I found Tamriko's teddy bear on the bedroom couch. Didn't Ia say she had taken everything? I kept wondering as I found several boxes full of Tamriko's toys. They hadn't taken anything. The house was filled to the brim with lifeless, useless things. I put the teddy bear on my bedside table. Sat on the bed: if I were to suffer so much, if my life was going to be so bitter, how could I have so easily discarded everything that had kept us going for so long? But where did that regret come from? Was I capable of forgiving Ia for cheating on me? Could I have gone on as if nothing had happened? Gone back to what we had even though we might have been slaves to the illusion called love? Nothing good comes out of sheer illusions. You just can't construct, imagine, or cling to something which should come on its own, naturally and effortlessly.

But still, what's wrong with me? Why do others find my composure so distressing? Among my other qualities, why do they single it out? Ana-Maria, for instance, told me at Turtle Lake that she liked calm people. But Ia screamed at me saying she hated my calmness. The trick is that neither of them is right—I'm far from being a calm person. Above all, it's not the feature that can make a woman clearly suffering from a nervous breakdown feel the bliss of tranquility, or send the other one, obviously on the verge of a fit, into a state of frenzy. My composure is an act, a ploy. My professional mask. The questions asked by my patients might sound abnormal, but are deeply human and only someone hiding behind the mask of composure can ward them off. In fact, one like myself has to lie to the patients because their questions have no answers because they are … so human! The great Greek said he didn't treat illness, he cured people instead. And because like many others I tend to forget the wise man's words, I have erected a lofty wall around myself, which means not only that it's impenetrable for others, but that my essence can't get out either, being confined within, unable to splash in the stormy waves of what's called Life, something so unattainable for us—people.

Those are my thoughts as I go in and out of the rooms, pacing like a bear in a cage. I dread the bed because I know it's going to become an instrument of torture. I miss Tamriko. Several days before they left, I remember sitting at the kitchen table. Tamriko trotted in and sat on my lap. Tamriko, I asked, do you love Daddy? She nodded. And Mummy? She shook her head. You're lying too, aren't you? And I kissed her hair smelling of herbs that no one can identify. All at once I started to cry. Tamriko joined me. Ia rushed into the kitchen. What have you done to the child, you conman! No, it wasn't a lie. Those were my first genuine tears since my childhood. I must have been overwhelmed by the smell of Tamriko's hair and I reacted in the least typical way, quite unexpected for my nature.

I was thinking of Tamriko but it was Ana-Maria who I visualized, which was not only inappropriate but rather vile on my part. Someone inside me — that other — much harsher and more relentless, was trying to remember the woman who I was striving to forget with as much effort and pain as a junkie going through withdrawal. The invariable scene of my dreams, which turned my sleep into agony, was a small wooden pier with a boat without oars. It indicated the existence of another, mysterious world with no name because in reality it didn't exist. And now, the nostalgia for that dreamy world had somehow made its way into reality, making my life absolutely unbearable. I'll go, I thought, and have a drink. I pitied both Tamriko and Ana-Maria, but I doubt there was anything to pity them for. I, on the other hand, had nowhere to go, no shelter for a refugee from one's solitude. I phoned my colleague: "Are you busy?"

"No, just helping the kid with Math."

"And can you?"

"Not really, but I've got to."

"Take pity on the child!"

"No choice for him either."

"Okay, I don't feel like your cynical jokes."

"I'm not joking. Do you feel that bad?"

"I do," I said, or rather blurted out, wondering how he sensed how bad I felt.

"It happens," he said.

"Fancy going out?"

"Like where?"

"For a drink. But not to our regular diner."

"No way!"

"Why?"

"At this time? There are two places in Tbilisi you can never get into — restaurants and public toilets. The former are overcrowded and the latter don't exist."

"Fine. Maybe next time."

"Yeah, maybe," he said and hung up.

I took the teddy bear from the bedside table: "Do you know Ana-Maria?" I asked it. "No? If you knew, if you only knew how lucky you are!" I kissed it on its muzzle and replaced on the table. I made another phone call: "Albina? Remember me? Can you come to my place? In half an hour? Fine, in half an hour."

She arrived in exactly thirty minutes. While we were climbing the stairs to the bedroom, she asked: "Did you miss me?"

I didn't reply, just slapped her on her bum. She giggled ... When she was putting on her boots, she told me I could call her whenever I felt like it. I heard her going down the stairs, thumping quite loudly. Our women only lift their feet in bed, my colleague used to say. Then the door closed with a bang ...

Several days passed and something I'd never expected to happen actually happened. It was already December. It brought some snow but only for a very short time, as if the winter had sent out scouts and recalled them almost immediately. The cold, though, was that of December. The clinic was freezing. The patients stayed in their beds. I had an old-fashioned oil heater in my office. It didn't so much heat as smoke and crackle a lot. My eyes hurt. "We can take care of things without you," my colleague and drinking companion told me. He suspected it was much warmer in my flat. Indeed, I had the luxury: as soon as we came back from Switzerland, we had a German heating system installed, with the help from my father-in-law of course. But the problem was I was afraid of staying alone at home. I felt as if the unbearable loneliness was waiting for me at home, crouching in ambush. That's why I used to linger, only getting home at bedtime when I had no choice but to go home. But you could hardly apply the word sleep to my nights. I dreaded falling asleep. As I said, my bed turned into a device of torture. I hardly ever took a book to to bed to read either.

It was about eight in the evening when I got home from the office. My doorbell buzzed. I opened the door and stood there, unable to utter a word out of utter surprise.

"Can I come in?" Ana-Maria asked with a smile.

"Please do. Please come in."

"You didn't expect me, did you?"

We were in the living room. She was pressing her coiled up red scarf to her breast.

"Please have a seat."

"No, thanks. I've only dropped in for a minute. A taxi's waiting outside. See what I've brought you! The taxi driver gave it to me. I just patted it and he said I could have it. And I want you to have it. It's a present." She had a puppy wrapped in her scarf. She crammed it into her pocket and held out the puppy. "Have a look. It's so cute!"

I took the puppy. Stroked it.

"Do you like dogs?" she asked.

"No, I don't," I answered. I was stroking the puppy while my eyes never left her face.

She was taken aback by my words: "I don't believe it!" She tried to smile.

She was wearing a short leather jacket with a white furry lining. A fluffy turtleneck sweater. Black pants (How tall she is! I thought) and thick-soled black boots that laced in front.

"Why are you staring?" she asked, this time smiling with her whole face.

"I'm trying to remember you," I replied.

"Have you forgotten how I look?"

"How could I?"

"I was going somewhere else but this little imp," she pointed at the puppy, "changed my plans, so I came here."

"Thanks for the present."

"I thought you'd be happy."

"Who says I'm not? What I don't like is that you're not sitting down. I'll make you coffee."

"No, thanks. I've got to go. Next time."

"What shall we call it?" I asked at the front door.

"If you have nothing against, let's call him Terry. I had a Terry when I was little. I loved him." She patted the puppy. "Terry, Terry, you little poor thing." She kissed him.

She was gone. Left me astounded. I stared at the door which was closed right in my face as if it would open again re-admitting Ana-Maria.

When she came the second time, she told me she was visiting Terry. In the meanwhile, I had become quite skilled in taking care of the dog. Brother, I told myself, you were born to be a handler, why did you choose to be a doctor for God's sake? Can't you see the world's full of dog-crazy people, or at least our canine friends are loved more than you are? You should have guessed by now! No, I didn't mean Ana-Maria. My irony was directed towards our society which treated each other so relentlessly. But is there a society at all? The first thing that vanished or died was the society, the sense of community. Now it's only shreds, faceless bits and pieces that flutter in the streets and parks. People are walking the pets bred over thousands of years, the pets which have long ago degenerated, forgetting they were initially designated to hunt and guard. Now they prefer to live like that, with chains round their necks, in time resembling their owners more than their ancestors. That's what I thought about when I used to get home after work, laden with the glossy packages of Royal Canine and Pedigree bought for Terry at the supermarket. I couldn't help memorizing all those brand names glowing at me from the high-quality multi-colored packaging. Why on earth, I sometimes thought, couldn't I take care of Tamriko? Why hadn't I even once struggled to have her in my care? In fact, it could've been relatively easy to make Ia leave the child with me. Not because she didn't love her but because she hated me.

"Have you given Terry away?" Ana-Maria asked me.

"Oh, no! How could I?"

"Then show me where he is."

I took her to the corner where I had put rags for the dog. They weren't rags though because I had used Ia's expensive clothes to make a comfortable bed for my expensive Terry. Enough to make any royal canine feel envious.

She knelt in the corner: "Come here," she took the puppy into her arms and kissed him. "Isn't he gorgeous?" she beamed at me.

I nodded. I was excited. My heart was thumping like mad. Suddenly I noticed her intense gaze.

"What are you looking at?" I asked.

"Is this the couch you use for your patients? Is this the famous psychiatrist's couch?"

"It is," I answered. "This is my study."

"I don't wish to be your patient," she whispered.

She was lost in thought, holding a tress of her hair with two fingers.

"Neither do I," I said, "and you won't be."

"But I am your patient, aren't I?"

"Would you like to take off your jacket? Thank god Russia gave us gas, so the heating's on."

She took off her jacket and put it on the chair.

"For as long as I can remember, even at the lyceum, I've always wanted to lie down on such a couch. In films women talk to their doctors reclining on similar couches. The movie stars. But I was scared." She carefully put the puppy down and sat on the chaise-longue.

"Scared?" I took a chair and pulled it closer to her.

"I was. Or rather I was embarrassed. I had nothing to tell. Or the way I lived seemed so unimportant, so unremarkable that I was reluctant to discuss it with a stranger or a doctor."

She leaned back.

"People should free themselves from unspoken words. It's the fossilized words stuck in one's soul that prevent us from creating a new life. And there's a fierce rivalry between that old or real life and the new one. That's why it's essential to get rid of those words. But in order to succeed, one needs an attentive, sensitive listener, which, I hope you agree is hard to find. Practically impossible considering our hectic and alienated life. Do I sound stupid?" she laughed.

"No. You make a lot of sense."

"A person lying on the couch can't talk gibberish because one tries to tell the truth, right? And the truth is always interesting. However, I feel it's not at all necessary to be truthful with the doctor. The main thing is to talk, the more the better, even if you're lying through your teeth. Actually, it's even preferable as you're helping the doctor better assess your condition." She talked to me propping her head on her arm. "Why are you looking at me like that?" she suddenly asked.

"I'm listening." I couldn't say I admired her every word and gesture, as if I was a proud parent watching and listening to one's kid.

She rose. Sat on my knees, put her arm round my neck and looked sideways at me.

"Are you insane too?" Her face was worried. Her eyes seemed to be darker and heavier. But only for a second. Then she laughed, got to her feet, and took a pack of cigarettes from her pocket. She lit one and asked me: "Did I frighten you?"

She crushed the cigarette in the ashtray and pulled her sweater over her head. She had nothing underneath. Something seemed to explode right there, in front of my eyes, but noiselessly.

"No," I whispered, "No, don't!"

She looked at me in surprise: "Don't you like me?"

"No, it's . . ." I muttered.

"I thought you did . . ."

"I love you!" I shouted. "Love you!"

"Why shout?" she asked in amazement.

Absurdly, I got angry, just like a teacher frustrated at being unable to explain even the simplest thing to a pupil.

"I love you," I repeated but very quietly, absolutely exhausted. Those couple of seconds seemed to have completely drained me as if

I had just finished physically demanding work. But more than that, I was stricken by a sudden realization that it was love that had kept me so miserable for such a long time. I had fallen in love for the first time in my life and this unexpected discovery nearly made me faint.

I came to my senses upstairs, in my bedroom. She was lying with her back to me. But she wasn't asleep. Easy to tell when one is sleeping. I had no recollection how we ended up in the bedroom, in my bed, how we climbed the stairs or how long I'd been nearly unconscious. My body, every inch of me, every tiny particle had a vivid memory of an unearthly pleasure, never experienced before. It was absolute bliss, victory of sheer natural elements over the mind. I was reminded of Yma Sumac who could produce the sounds of nature's orgasm. The transfixed audience would listen to groans, shouts, moans, and gurgles—the accompaniment of the best human act, which was evenly shared among the listeners hushed like a praying congregation in church. I leaned over and kissed her between her shoulder blades. I got up, put on my dressing-gown and slippers, and went downstairs.

I was making coffee and remembering my own lyrical lines: the aroma of your body makes me dizzy, reminding me of a tree from the Garden of Eden which isn't listed in any botanical reference. The aroma has stayed with Eve ever since and is inherited only by true women. These were the lines I wrote many years ago in my diary, believed to have been well forgotten. I was surprised I still remembered. Hadn't forgotten a single word. As if the phrases finally found their true addressee, a true owner. Yes, my miserable scribbling of my younger days now belonged to Ana-Maria. The lines inspired by an inexplicable prophecy seemed to have waited for this very day, this very minute.

I made the coffee. Poured it into a cup. Took a sip. And burnt my mouth. It was absolutely essential to feel I was back to reality.

"Are you praying?" Ana-Maria had crept downstairs unnoticed.

"Kind of. You can't make really good coffee without a bit of magic, can you? Do you want some?"

"No, thanks. I've had time to shower."

She was wrapped in a fluffy bathrobe and was drying her hair with a towel.

"Do you really love me so much?" She didn't wait for my reply. She wasn't interested, fully confident in what I would say. "Just look at this!" she cried. "Look at all the clothes!" Our clothes were strewn all over the room and the stairs. Unwittingly, we seemed to be in a desperate hurry to get rid of all kind of hindrance. "My goodness, how many things one wears! An experienced forensic expert can follow our trail to the crime scene just as he'd trace blood stains."

"Crime?" I was startled by the word.

"You don't think so?" she asked in return. "Don't you think we're offenders? I as a wife and you as a doctor who's sinned with his patient."

I smiled: "I'd like to be judged by someone who looks at you and doesn't desire you at least in his thoughts."

I pulled the bathrobe off her and lost my mind again, this time on the kitchen table cleared with my sleeve ... Later, when we were standing together under the shower, she smiled at me:

"Do you remember I said I didn't see you as my doctor?"

"I do, of course I do."

"I believe you were offended at the time."

"I wasn't. I was just stunned by your prophecy."

"Which means you haven't sinned. Actually, is there anything sweeter than sin in the world?"

Before leaving, she asked after Terry.

"There he is," I pointed.

He was under the table.

She bent down and slapped her knees.

"Terry, come here! Come here, you little imp!"

Like a cotton wool ball, Terry wobbled toward us. His little legs slipped on the floor.

"He's so funny! So cute!" She cuddled him, pressed him to her breast, "Terry, Terry, poor imp."

Several days passed without a word from her. Instead, Lulu called me, which was really unexpected.

"Hello, Doctor. How are you?"

"Fine, thank you, Lulu. Thank you indeed."

"I'm pleased you recognized me. It's quite a while since you last phoned us, which we take as a favorable sign. Does it mean Ana-Maria doesn't need any treatment?"

"Ana-Maria never needed any professional treatment," I replied. "Ana-Maria is absolutely healthy."

"It's good to hear it from a doctor like you."

I noticed she had mentioned my profession several times.

Meanwhile, Lulu went on: "I'd like you to know we strictly follow your advice. I take her to Turtle Lake in the mornings. She likes the place and insists on going there. And in the evenings she strolls up and down the street in front of the Embassy. Alone."

She seemed to have stressed the word. I said: "Excellent. She should keep on. Everyone benefits from long walks in the fresh air."

"Thank you, Doctor."

"If you think it necessary," I said and immediately sensed I was overdoing it. She could have thought I was addressing her in her capacity of a warden. That's exactly what must have happened as I halted for a minute and she allowed the pause to drag on without interruption. After a moment her firm voice sounded in my ear: "Yes, Doctor?"

"You can call me anytime," I managed to say.

"Thank you, Doctor. Good-bye."

The conversation left a sour aftertaste. It agitated and worried me. Why would Lulu phone me? What was her true purpose? Was I being warned? I didn't know ... Anyway, I had to take the call as a kind of warning because I failed to find any other explanation even though I tried very hard. I might have read too much into it because of my agitation, but I was pretty sure Lulu would have never phoned just to ask about my well-being. It might have been better if I mentioned Ana-Maria had dropped in a couple of times for a consultation, though I wasn't at all obliged to report everything to Lulu in detail. She probably knew about Ana-Maria's visits. Not probably, certainly. That's exactly why I had to interpret her phone call as a warning. But would it make any difference? I could have easily made our relationship public and married Ana-Maria. Those were my thoughts and they didn't frighten me. Deep down, I was confident it would never happen, just couldn't happen. Only an extremely naïve person could imagine such an outcome of our relationship. Naïve and ... immoral! How could I decide the future of our—hers and mine—lives without her? The best solution was to follow the course of events, neither hasten nor slow down the natural flow. In truth, I wasn't in the least sure our relationship was going to continue at all! I suspected she could easily shift from being utterly daring to impenetrably self-restrained. It seemed to be an abnormal passion of a completely normal woman. Even in my thoughts I couldn't make myself call it love! But could such powerful passion be abnormal? Could it be love and nothing else but love? Actually, more often than not we see things as abnormal or believe they are abnormal only because we are unable to do them or they are absolutely unattainable for us!

As soon as I hung up, my colleague called me: "Well done, pal! You've got yourself a really smashing woman. They say she's got no match in Tbilisi."

"What do you mean? Who told you that crap?" My heart sank. "Who told you?"

"Tbilisi is a small village, pal. No secrets. But if you take my advice, it won't do you any good to fall for a beautiful woman. They tend to look in the mirror with their bums."

God! That was sheer mystique! Only a handful of people had seen me with Ana-Maria and I was pretty sure they didn't even know me in person. I remember every one of them, can even name them: the guard at the Embassy, the Niva driver who was changing tires, the waiter, the gypsy girl ... What was her name? Era. Who else? No, no one else had seen us together. My colleague must have heard weird rumors, nothing serious. Had he known about other, more delicate things, he would have certainly told me so. How could he miss the chance! Just imagine—the Ambassador's wife is the mistress of a Tbilisi doctor! Fit to feature in a Mexican soap opera! Ana-Maria and I hadn't been anywhere else except Turtle Lake. I was completely lost. The initial shock wore off as I began to gradually realize this "rumor" wasn't threatening for either Ana-Maria or me. Unlike my first reaction. We had gone to Turtle Lake not only with the lady's husband's consent but at his request!

Everything became clear when, in one of our conversations not connected to the problem, my colleague told me his elder daughter worked in the information section of the Embassy. I immediately guessed "the rumors" had seeped out of the Embassy itself. The colleague's daughter of course knew me and my frequent calls must have attracted her attention, especially because she was kept in the dark about the circumstances regarding how I had met the Ambassador's wife in the first place. She could have thought I was just a likable philanderer, if one could put these two notions side by side. She might have even sympathized with Ana-Maria and me. There's no stopping feminine imagination, I thought and added, but it could be amazingly precise as well! The girl might have made up the whole "romance" and shared her suspicions with her father, who his family considered to be my best friend. That could have been the explanation for the entire intrigue, but I might have been wrong ... Who'd tell me the truth?

"I've been here many times already and I keep telling you more or less the same story. As time goes by, I begin to suspect I've made the whole thing up. But there was a baby, wasn't there? And I'm getting to the point of today's visit. I saw you last at the Embassy reception. The invitations were printed by our company." Nunu took the hair hanging down her forehead in her two fingers and looked at Levan.

"Why do you look at me like that?" Levan asked after a short pause.

"Do I remind you of anyone you know?"

Of course he immediately pictured Ana-Maria, but didn't show it: "Who exactly? And yes, I was at that reception."

"Someone who's been visiting you quite often recently ..."

"I've got many patients. Why don't you drop the mysterious veil and be direct?" By then he was absolutely confident Nunu meant Ana-Maria. He was quite ready to hear her name but Nunu came up with a completely unexpected remark: "I'm talking about my daughter!"

"Excuse me?" Levan was taken aback.

"I knew it was her the moment I saw her. She's got it from me," she took a tress of hair in two fingers. "Initially she attracted my attention because she was talking to you. My heart already knew but I became sure when I followed her down the garden path. I found it hard to stay focused. My heart was beating really fast. She approached some men, standing with her back to me. The desire to embrace and kiss her nearly choked me. I wanted to hug her as if she were a baby, something I'd never done, but the burning desire had clearly lived in me all those years, dozing deep in my soul, awaking at that very minute. In my entire life I'd never felt anything like that before though, believe me, I'd seen many babies, held and cuddled them, even kissed many cute ones—but what I felt that day in the garden was extraordinary. I sat down on a bench. 'Do you feel all right?' A man asked who was sitting next to me. There were others on the bench, talking to each other, but I didn't notice them in my haste to sit down. As I told you I nearly fainted. 'Aaaaaa,' I sang as if I was rocking a baby in my arms. 'Madam?' The man next to me sounded genuinely worried. 'It's nothing, I'm fine,' I came to my senses. I smiled, 'I'm sorry, I believe I've disturbed you. Please forgive me.' I rose to my feet but the men sprang up first. By then I could stand firmly on my own, but I sat back down on the bench. I kept looking at her. Several times she glanced at you. You were still standing at the bar where you talked and where I first saw her. You had two empty glasses in your hands and were furtively looking at her too. See, you've done me another great favor—you helped me find my daughter!"

"Your daughter?"

"Now you think I've really lost my mind, don't you?" She guessed quite precisely what Levan was thinking. "Since then I can say I have turned into her shadow. I followed her in Gela's car because she used to drive. True, it didn't happen often. In a month she left the Embassy only a couple of times. By then I already knew she was the Ambassador's wife, had no children, and I knew who she visited in the city. I can tell you with absolute confidence she didn't visit anyone but you. You should've guessed by now who I'm talking about."

"I have," Levan said. And couldn't help thinking the rumors had really spread rather fast and wide.

"I'd like you to know I'm extremely happy she's coming to you."

"As I've already said, many patients visit my place." Levan began to sound annoyed. But she hastily added: "I don't want her to be your patient!" She even made an impatient gesture with her hand, as if wishing to deny the possibility, unsure the words were enough. "I just don't want that!" Then she added in a softer voice, even meekly, "Does she really need a doctor? Does she?"

When Levan hesitated with his reply, Nunu exclaimed, bright-faced: "See! I told you, didn't I?"

"Told me what?" Levan asked. He felt his usual composure was failing him.

"I want you to love her," she said rather quietly and lit another cigarette. "You come across as an extremely decent person."

"You're saying strange things," Levan told her.

"I'm a mother!" she exclaimed.

"A mother?"

"You're right, I might not be the best one and hardly deserve the honor of being called a mother, but God knows it wasn't my fault. God is perfectly aware of the circumstances. I believe I've already told you that things come true for me but in a kind of weird way. That's how it is with me. I even became a mother! There's hardly a woman in the world who doesn't want to be a mother, but not my way. I'll tell you more, something even stranger. I found her after all those years …"

"Are you sure she's your daughter?" Levan asked, calmly this time.

"Absolutely!" she exclaimed emotionally and repeated, "Absolutely! But I feel nothing towards her except … I'm embarrassed to say it but I still will, except curiosity! And pride! Don't be surprised—a woman can be proud of another woman's beauty but that one has to be her daughter. See, I can joke about it? Amazing how freely I can talk to you, be completely relaxed. Your serenity has an extremely positive effect on me. It was the same twenty-seven years ago when I was put in your clinic and I met you. I've always remembered you and felt something drew me to you. Nothing in this world is accidental and it's not accidental that I chose you to tell my story to. I don't mean the narrative I was obliged to repeat over and over again. You helped me find my daughter. Since then I've been waiting at the Embassy for her to come out. I follow her. But I dare not approach her and talk to her. I just can't brace myself for it. It takes more than I've got. In truth, I need to discuss extremely important things with her. In this period she visited an antiquity shop in Marjanishvili Street several times, went to the symphony twice, once to the Conservatory and another time to the new Music Centre. Yes, and once she went to the Rustaveli Drama Theatre together with a black lady. That's all, at least her official visits as far as she was driven by the Embassy car to all those places. Oh, nearly forgot—she strolls round Turtle Lake every morning. And the only unofficial route she takes leads here, to your place! She always takes a taxi for these visits. A couple of times she got out of the taxi but changed her mind about seeing you and drove away practically immediately. What I'm trying to say is that she visits you more often than any other place. In the beginning I thought she was seeing a psychiatrist and, by coincidence, the person was you, my first doctor! The realization made me smile—the mother and daughter had something in common." She was quiet, lit a cigarette, and smoked it greedily.

"Why are you telling me all this?" Levan asked.

"Do you take me for a blackmailer?" she asked in turn.

"Oh, no! Of course not, but ..."

"I'm not going to blackmail you, so you needn't get upset."

"I'm not upset."

"There's no reason to be because it's none of my business why she visits you ..."

Levan thought the woman might be truly insane.

In the meantime Nunu took a metal dog tag from her handbag.

"When I was transferred from here to the clinic in Moscow, they returned my personal belongings. They told me I had a golden chain with a cross and this one round my neck. It took me some time to remember the reason I wore this dog tag together with my cross—I'd taken it off the man who came down from the sky before I buried him and had worn it ever since. Once my husband asked me what I kept in the left luggage room to wear the token at all times. I said he was rather cynical, didn't I? It does look like a cloakroom token. Strange, but it feels as if I really left something somewhere, the trouble is I don't know exactly what or where." She smiled. "You must think I've lost my mind, right? I know it's quite typical for the unbalanced to claim they found their lost children. The obsession is so strong that they chase them everywhere. But that's not the case with me, please trust me. Do you think I look like a maniac?" She didn't wait for the answer, clearly uninterested in what Levan had to say and continued, "That's why I came to see you." She finished and stared at Levan.

"Please go on. I'm listening."

"Excuse me?" she came back from her reverie. "Ah, yes, where was I? My request is to pass this dog tag to her, please. I've got no courage to go near her and explain things she needs to know. Please tell her it once belonged to her father so she must have it. But she should keep it a secret. Under no circumstances should she show it to anyone because I don't wish my daughter to share my fate. However, I predict her life will be much, much worse if she decides to disclose its existence to anyone. You've got my complete trust because you're a noble soul. Oh, I'll show you something!" She took a photo from her handbag and handed it to Levan: Ana-Maria was standing at a car, holding a tress of hair in two fingers. She was smiling. "She's smiling at me!"

"Did you get so close to her?"

"I took it with my mobile and thanked her. She waved to me. What could I do? Rush to her and say I was her mother? Tell her everything from the start? The things I spent ten years in clinics or prisons for?" She rose to her feet. "I must be going. I'm sorry for disturbing you."

"I'll call for a taxi. It's rather late," Levan saw her to the front door.

"No, thanks, don't worry. Gela's waiting for me."

In the photo she looked exactly like I remembered her from our first meeting. At the Embassy reception. By an uncanny coincidence she came by that same day.

"How are you, boys?"

"Terry and I are fine, thanks," I answered.

"Come on, say you've missed me."

"Of course we did."

She lifted Terry and cuddled him.

"Are you well looked after, baby?"

"I thought you'd left," I said. "I haven't seen you for so long."

"I haven't gone anywhere. I just couldn't get out. Don't forget I'm married."

"How can I forget it?" I laughed.

"This time I've just dropped in for a minute."

"To see Terry, I suppose," I said.

"A taxi's waiting." She put Terry down very carefully. "Take care. And here are my kisses," she blew at her palm sending Terry and me kisses. "Must be going. Behave yourselves."

I stopped her at the door:

"Wait a sec. I've got something for you."

"You needn't get angry," she said with a smile.

"Angry?" I was surprised. In truth I was. "Just a second. I'll get it." I brought an envelope with the dog tag.

"What's that?"

"I don't know. A woman asked me to pass it to you. Said it belonged to you."

"What woman?"

"Does it matter? You don't know her anyway. She insisted you don't show it to anyone."

"One of your patients?"

"No, believe it or not. However, I'd think the same if I were in your shoes. Sorry, I can't say more."

"Fine. And thanks." She stuffed the envelope in her pocket. "Here's a kiss." She kissed me on the cheek. "Aren't you going to kiss me?"

"No," I said. "The taxi's waiting."

"Okay, I'm off. Terry, have fun. I'll be back. Bye," she said and was gone.

Several days later she came at night. When she rang the doorbell, I was asleep, but being a light sleeper, I heard it at once. I turned on the lights and checked the time. It was two in the morning. The doorbell sounded again, but very quietly this time as if the unexpected visitor knew I wasn't asleep but was trying to hurry me up a little. I got up. Went downstairs, wrapping my robe and tying the belt. I wasn't used to late visits.

"Who's there?" I asked the door which had no peep-hole. The door was a present to my father from a grateful patient. It came complete with workers who, despite dad's protests, unhinged the old one and installed the new one. It was heavy as a church door, the donor said at the time, smiling suspiciously. The bell rang again. I opened the door.

"Ana-Maria?" I couldn't hide my worry. I expected anyone but Ana-Maria at this time of the night.

"Will you let me in?"

She came in.

She had a short black sports jacket on and a backpack whose two straps she clutched in both hands. A smaller bag hung over her shoulder.

"You look like a parachute jumper," I smiled at her.

She drew up a chair and sat down, took a pack of Camel's from her jacket pocket, lit a cigarette, and blew out the words together with the smoke: "I'm going to jump!"

Her face was strangely tense as if she was trying to smile but couldn't manage it. She was either cold or in pain. I went nearer and sat down facing her.

"Look at me."

"I am," she said but didn't look up.

"What's wrong?" I was getting uneasy with worry.

She didn't reply.

"Why don't you take off your jacket? It's warm here."

She didn't react. After a long pause she asked: "What's the time?" She seemed to be addressing someone else because she didn't look at me. Simply stared into space.

I didn't answer. I guessed she wasn't really interested.

"I'll take it off if I may," she said.

"I've just asked you to. Why ask again?"

She put her shoulder bag on the floor, then took off her jacket and dropped it on the bag.

"By the way," she said, "I have jumped from a plane. But only once. I'd lie if I said I enjoyed it. I wasn't scared though. If I were, I'd never have done it. I seemed to be lost in the infinite mysterious void, but I didn't belong there anyway. I was a complete stranger, like a gatecrasher." She lit another cigarette. "Just like I am here now."

I allowed a little anger to creep into my voice: "What are you saying? Can you hear yourself?"

She again tried to smile: "I was joking."

"Why don't you tell me what's wrong? What happened?"

"You didn't expect me, did you?" She bent forward, leaning her elbows on the table. "Did you?"

"I didn't," I replied. "You've never come so late."

"Have you got anyone in there?" she indicated the bedroom upstairs with her eyes.

"Is that another joke?"

"It is. Daft, I guess. Sorry."

"You'd better tell me what happened. But if you don't want to, don't."

"I'd rather we sat like this," she said. "Can you make me coffee? If I knew the right magic words, I'd do it myself, but I'm no good at it, just like at joking."

I went upstairs, got dressed, and came down again.

"Have you forgotten about the coffee?" she asked.

"I haven't," I answered. "In a second. That's the easy part."

"Remember I dropped in the other day?" she asked after a while. "I know you sulked because I just came for a minute, but I really couldn't stay longer. You gave me a metal dog tag, remember? Can you tell me who gave it to you?"

"I don't know," I lied. "I don't know the woman. She just stopped me in the street and asked me to pass it on to you."

"How did she know you knew me?"

"No idea. Can't say anything about it."

"Once, I told you, if you recall, that sometimes I dream when I'm not sleeping and that day, when I got home, it happened again. It felt like living in two realities inserted into one another, like floating on stinging waves. I walked and talked, took a bath, but I kept hearing a strange sound, which had a kind of hypnotic effect on me. I was unable to do anything, make even the simplest decisions. Being powerless and dependent on the invisible mysterious force drove me crazy but calmed me down at the same time—if one can imagine madness and tranquility side by side. That's how I felt—calmly crazy. It must've been only me who heard the guiding voice of my consciousness. Like a sleepwalker, I was drawn to it which was not only hard but absolutely impossible because I was trapped in a web of sounds fragmented into countless particles. At times I believed the sound had been with me all my life, had in fact been born with me. Suddenly I remembered about the dog tag. I rushed to my jacket, took out the envelope and opened it—it was the metal tag that was producing the buzzing sound. Not only buzzing but talking to me. The language of the dog tag was unlike anything familiar though I know many languages. I understood the 'buzzing language' perfectly well as if it were French or my native Swedish. Please, don't take my story as complete madness."

All of a sudden I was gripped by fear. My body was saturated by an inexplicable foresight, as if it were a sponge. It wasn't an ordinary fear, not even the dread of death. I felt under the total control of an overpowering sensation of helplessness, which also seemed to block my mind. I was stunned by the sudden turn of the hitherto unrealistic story, taken as a fantasy concocted by an irrational mind, impelling me to see it in a completely new light.

I excused myself, saying I'd be back in a minute. I went into the bathroom and splashed some cold water on my face.

"What's wrong with you?" I asked my reflection in the mirror.

No, it wasn't a commonplace fear. It was a premonition of something dreadful, an alarm sounded by my intuition and common sense.

I went back into the room: "Give me a cigarette!" I reached for her pack.

"What's come over you?" she asked in surprise but handed me the pack.

"Nothing, nothing." I took a cigarette from it. She held her lighter. "Thanks. Nothing." I repeated. I seemed to be regaining my senses. I nearly shouted, "I said nothing!" When I met with her astonished, rounded eyes, I apologized. "I'm sorry. Please, don't pay attention." For some reason I calmed down instantly, but oddly enough I had the same vision of myself I had pictured several months earlier when

I felt really miserable—me in an old man's armchair, wrapped in a warm plaid, taking a cigarette to my mouth with a shaking hand. It touches my lip. I smell and taste tobacco. I roll its tiny particle on my tongue. I suck at it as if it were a heart pill.

Ana-Maria was sitting with her head bent low, staring at her hands on the table. She must have been speaking but I missed it because my hearing seemed to be coming back very slowly. All the while I was wondering what scared me so much. It was unbelievable anyway. Nothing of the kind could happen in reality.

Ana-Maria was silent, debating whether to say it or not. Finally she did: "I showed the dog tag to my husband."

"No!" I uttered.

"I was obliged to." She must have guessed my reaction and added, "You're right. You warned me not to show it to anyone, but ..."

I felt oddly relieved. Till then I doubted I had warned her about keeping it a secret.

"It had slipped my mind he planned to go hunting that day. Before leaving he looked into my room. As a rule he seldom does it. The dog tag was on the table, buzzing as usual. He asked what it was. I said I heard it. He asked what exactly I heard. I said I could hear it talk. He stared at me in amazement. I said for some reason I believed it talked to me. He put the dog tag to his ear and asked if it buzzed like that all the time. I answered only when it was close to me. He sent me out of the room for a minute. I went out and returned shortly. 'What does it say? What's the language?' I said I didn't know what exactly it was but I understood it perfectly well. 'It says they're looking for me and will definitely find me soon.' He took the tag and asked me for permission to take it away. He came back several hours later and said, 'When I came earlier I wanted to tell you about your mother. I had a phone call from Paris.' 'Is she alive?' I was worried. He said she was in a clinic. I asked why I wasn't called to the phone, but he explained I was still asleep and he decided not to wake me up. I rushed to the phone. No one answered the landline one. I guessed everyone was in the clinic. I said I wanted to leave immediately. He agreed I should do so. When I asked where my dog tag was, he didn't reply but asked in his turn how I came to have it. I said an unknown woman had stopped me in the street and given it to me in an envelope. I gave him the envelope and he put it into his pocket. Then he spoke with deliberation, very distinctly, as if a teacher talking to a student. He warned me it was top secret. He said he had sent the dog tag to the Department and already received their initial reaction. They said the metal the tag was made from wasn't found on our planet. After a pause he added it was obvious the tag was given to the rightful owner because he had witnessed it 'talk' to me. I whispered, 'We remember you, we wait for you, we're going to find you.' He interrupted me, warning to forget it. 'Forget what?' I asked. He told me not to discuss its existence with anyone. I was scared. Also the Department wanted to know how the strange object ended up with him. 'I explained a woman crammed an envelope into my hand. At the time I thought it was another criticism of the government,' he said. I wanted to know why they didn't ask how he decided the dog tag was extraordinary. 'Why haven't they asked you the reason you sent it to them immediately?' He said they know—that's what Lulu was for in the Embassy, an expert in mysteries. 'The moment she saw it, she guessed it was alien metal. Incidentally, don't let her know you've ever seen it or even know it exists.' He made sure I understood what he said. I was about to ask why he made such an effort to warn me about the secrecy, but he seemed to predict my query, saying, 'Because you're my wife.' He paused, so I asked if he'd finished. To which he said, 'I love you!' He'd never said it before. I felt I had inadvertently got myself into something unpleasant or even dangerous. 'Don't scare me.' 'Are you scared of my love?' he laughed, rather tensely though and when I didn't reply, he went on, 'Don't be afraid but ...' He didn't finish, probably avoided repeating himself. We sat quietly for quite some time. He must have wished to add something but was reluctant. After some deliberation he braced himself to say, 'Now you're going to hear, Ana-Maria, something I've kept from you for a very long time for the simple reason that it wouldn't have affected our relationship, but might have hurt you. And now, when your mother is dying ...' 'Why didn't you wake me up?' I screamed and tears came streaming from my eyes. 'Don't cry. Please, listen to me. Maybe you'll hear the truth for once.' 'Is my dad dying too?' 'Of course not! I talked to him.' Like a fool, I kept asking why he hadn't woken me up, but he didn't pay attention, saying he might relieve my pain with what he had to tell me. 'Go on! Say it! Don't torture me!' I screamed. I sensed he was going to tell me something absolutely terrible, otherwise why was he hesitating? I was right when he started by saying, 'I'm only trying to ease your mind ...' 'Say it! Please!' I was already begging. Eventually, he managed to get it out, 'In the Department archive there is an application from your parents asking for permission to adopt a child in the Soviet Union. They planned to go to the 1980 Olympic Games.' I seemed to have lost my voice. The ability to speak came back some time later. 'Was that possible?' I whispered. 'Possible, but only unofficially.' Then I asked if he got the information from the Department. He said he had known it from the day we met. 'In other words, you've been gathering material on me,' I attempted to smile. 'I was obliged to, considering my job ...' I interrupted him, saying it was enough. 'I thought it'd ease your pain,' he repeated. I said I was wrong thinking I knew him. When he asked why I said so, I answered, 'Dear Henri, apparently you were devoid of childhood!' Then I blurted out, directly and rather insensitively, 'You probably know about the lad I loved before I met you. I was pregnant twice from him but miscarried. God must have decided I didn't deserve to have anyone really close, someone I could call my own. Exactly in the same way as I've just learnt that my parents, even my parents aren't my own!' He calmly replied he was aware of Jean Paul. 'Yes, Jean Paul, who really loved me! Which is so rare in this world. We believe we are loved, we think we can get through, but this elixir is just another myth!' He said quietly he knew that too. I went on, asking if he knew his wife had a lover. I hate the word but couldn't find a better one. The lover who loves me or at least I believe so. 'Did you know that?' I yelled. He was about to answer but changed his mind. He rose and went out. I never suspected I could speak to him so directly, so openly. Someone else seemed to be shouting those words. I'm not so cruel by nature. Oh, God! Life is so strange—we consider the truth to be cruel! What made me lose my balance was that someone, even if it was my husband, thought to help me regain peace of mind by saying my mother wasn't really the one who sat by my bed when I was little, sang lullabies, read bedtime stories to me, and now is dying alone, in complete solitude. While I'm miles away!"

She was silent for some time. Deep in thoughts of her own. Then she asked if I had any wine. I brought some and poured it into a glass. She sipped a little. In fact, only wet her lips.

"The Embassy was practically deserted. The men had gone hunting to Kakheti. For the whole weekend. I went down to the kitchen for supper, or rather for a cup of coffee. Lulu was there. She was the only other one living in the Embassy except us. Other staff rent flats in the city. Of course I don't mean the local staff. Lulu had a cup of coffee in front of her and was smoking a cigarette. I poured myself some. For a long time we sat without uttering a word. Then she said, 'I'm sorry to hear about your mother. Everything's ready—the ticket and papers.' I thanked her. She said she was simply carrying out my husband's instructions. 'He sends his apologies for not seeing you off as he couldn't cancel the hunting trip. There are others waiting for him in Kakheti. They've got a collective license to hunt game. I'll see you to the airport,' she added. I said I didn't need it as I was perfectly capable of finding my own way. She said the flight was at five in the morning and there was a car waiting to take me. I thanked her again and if she had nothing else to say, I wanted to get upstairs to pack. 'Who said I've got nothing else to say?' she stopped me at the door. I went back and sat down facing her. Lulu put a thick envelope in front of me. It was full of photos. The moment I glanced at the first one, I dropped the envelope as if I was bitten by a venomous snake. I think you've guessed the nature of those photos. Here, I've brought one." She took a photo from her bag and handed it to me. Smiling happily, she was hugging Terry in it. "Can you imagine they've been taking our pictures?"

"But how? Where is it taken?" I asked Ana-Maria.

"An unexpected question coming from you," she shook her head.

"Where could they take the photo of Terry and me together? Haven't you guessed Terry and you are the same?" She smiled, waving the smoke away. "You're pretty daft, my dear psychiatrist!" She put the photo back into her bag. "I'll pat him, my Levan, my Levan …"

A disgusting worm of fear dozing somewhere deep in my heart suddenly swelled, grew so big that it seemed there was another me stuffed inside my body, much larger than me, causing unbearable pain as a result.

"Yes but …" I couldn't manage more.

"Yes," Ana-Maria was fast picking up where I failed, "it must've been a hidden camera, watching both of us, or rather the three of us. Terry's another porn star." She turned to me, "What's the time?"

I said it was three.

"Ah, we've got all the time in the world! I asked Lulu if my husband knew we were photographed. She said no, Henri hadn't seen them. I congratulated her on their quality. They must've been taken by an expert. She thanked me without changing the expression of her face. That was when she emptied a bowl of fruit onto the table, put the negatives, photos, and the envelope into it and set fire to them all. I shouted not to burn just one and grabbed the one with Terry, saying I'd like to keep it as a memento."

She got to her feet, paced the room for a while, looked at Terry, saying how cute he was sleeping and how she'd love to sleep next to him on the rags. Then she took her mobile from her pocket and dialed a number.

"Are you awake, Agu? I knew you'd be. You're a disgusting black bat, but an extremely beautiful one. Yeah, it's me, Ana-Maria—a white, ugly heron. Will you take me to the airport? Yes, we had a row. What's good or funny about it? Yeah, I'll tell you all about it, in detail. I promise. Be a little patient. You thought I was much smarter? See, how wrong people can be, even the wisest Africans? Anyway, here's where I am," she dictated my address. "Be here at four sharp, okay? The plane's at five. Will we be on time? What, are you offended? Sorry, I forgot I'm talking to a female Schumacher. I'm waiting then. See you, bye."

Ana-Maria came back to the table and sat down: "She's an ambassador's wife too. We are colleagues, in a way. Incidentally, she was there, at the garden reception, where we met each other. You can't have missed a barefooted black girl. She got the beauty prize that evening."

I didn't tell her that evening I saw no one except her. Somehow I was embarrassed to admit it. It was true though.

"I can't wait to tell her what happened. She believes my husband and I had a serious row. Did you know that female friendship is based on curiosity? Why are you so quiet?"

"I'm listening," I said.

She lit a cigarette.

"When Lulu saw me with the bags, she asked where I was going because it was still pretty early for the airport and the car would be picking me up later. I answered she knew perfectly well where I was heading because I wanted to say goodbye. But I did ask her one thing—I didn't want her to mention your name, ever. Oh, by the way, do you remember the name of the girl we met at Turtle Lake? The one who was scared of me. Or have you forgotten too?"

"I do remember her very well," I replied. "She was a smart girl, but as for her name … I'm afraid I can't recall it."

She pointed her finger at me: "Incidentally, now it's you who's afraid of me. Am I right?"

I didn't say anything.

"Can you imagine that Jean Paul was the only one who really loved me? He died of a broken heart at the airport. But isn't it enough?" She was silent for a time and then asked, "Did you love me?" then added sternly, "No, don't say anything! I don't want to hear it! Remember what I asked you the very first time I came here? Do you? I asked you if we could just sit, without speaking. Let's do it now, shall we? Especially now that we've used up the available stock of words. To the last one. It's over and finished."

It was true. Women are clairvoyants. I also noticed that absolute indifference and apathy had taken the place of the previous fright. In other words, now I was completely indifferent. But at the same time, my awakened common sense had also brought along an ironic vision of myself too. I must have been the only man in human history who not only knew an alien woman but was probably loved by her. How else could this farewell scene be explained? Now it was paramount to find the strength in me to stay human to the end, or at least pretend to be. However, I also questioned if common sense meant justification of one's miserable existence. "One defeat!" I suddenly uttered. It surprised me immensely. Why did I say it out loud? What did it mean? What did I intend it to convey?

Ana-Maria looked at me in amazement: "What was that?"

"No idea," I said honestly.

She stared at me for some time, then averted her eyes and said: "I won't be coming back. All I want now is to see Mother before it's too late."

That very moment I told her what was nothing else but the courage of a cowardly, and not extremely honest, man, which is characteristic of cowardice: "I don't love you, Ana-Maria," I began quietly, speaking in a quivering voice, gradually raising it. "But Heaven knows I thought, I believed I loved you! I was happy!"

I immediately realized I was repeating the same grave mistake her husband had made when, with the intention of relieving her pain, he said her mother wasn't her biological mother. Appalled by my own treachery, I was already shouting I had been happy over and over again. She watched me in astonishment while I kept repeating "I was happy!" just to ease the pain of defeat for her. What's more, I actually believed in what I said or shouted at her. In this case, if anyone was deceived, it was me ... But happy! No, in fact unhappy from being happy! Apparently, one can't be completely happy if one doesn't fool oneself! I seemed to have a thorny ball stuck in my throat. It pushed its way upwards, threatening to tear me apart but, worse than that, all the while, as I kept saying the same phrase, I was thinking about an absolutely different thing—Tamriko! I've got to get her back! I've got to get my Tamriko back! The thought was choking me and in order not to suffocate, I voiced it. It was unexpected and its suddenness drained me of all strength. I leaned back on the chair, absolutely exhausted, panting as if I'd been running a marathon ...

For a while we sat without uttering a word. I was already capable of rational thinking. Defeated in the most decisive battle, battered, having fled the battlefield, I was already looking for a haven in which to lick my wounds.

She tapped her wrist with her finger, silently asking about the time. I said it was nearly four. She rose to her feet, saying it was time to go. She put her jacket on, lifted her bag, and heaved it over her back.

"Is that all your luggage?" I asked.

"Yeah. I managed to cram all my possessions into this backpack. I've taken the things I love. The Brueghel album you gave me among them, by the way."

Not long ago I had thoroughly searched the house looking for it. I didn't remember I'd given it to Ana-Maria.

"Thank you," I said.

"What for?"

"For taking the album with you." I was about to add something because I felt it was wrong to let her go like that but she was faster: "When Terry wakes up, kiss him for me."

A car signaled outside, giving a short and gentle hoot.

"That's what I call punctuality!" She went to the front door and stopped. "Please, don't see me off. I hate farewells." She seemed to hint I not even offer to accompany her to the airport. "Goodbye."

She rushed out.

Leaving the door wide open.

I looked outside. Caught sight of the car driving away. And of the tire tracks, darkly glistening, gradually disappearing under the softly falling snow.

I sat down on the porch. Stayed there, with the open door behind me, for a long time. I didn't feel the cold. Then Terry wobbled out, wagging his tail and whimpering. I lifted and cuddled him. He closed his eyes.

"Poor you, poor you," I kept telling him, "poor you ..."

GEORGIAN LITERATURE SERIES

The Georgian Literature Series aims to bring to an English-speaking audience the best of contemporary Georgian fiction. Made possible thanks to the financial support of the Georgian National Book Centre and the Ministry of Culture and Monument Protection of Georgia, the Series began with four titles, officially published in January 2014. Available in January 2015 are four new titles, offering readers a choice of Georgian literary works.

www.dalkeyarchive.com

GEORGIAN LITERATURE SERIES

Erlom Akhvlediani
Vano and Niko & other stories / Translated by Mikheil Kakabadze
Akhvlediani's minimalist prose pieces are Kafkaesque parables presenting individual experience as a quest for the other. ISBN 978-1-62897-106-4 / $15.95 US

Lasha Bugadze
The Literature Express / Translated by Maya Kiasashvili
The Literature Express is a riotous parable about the state of literary culture, the European Union, and our own petty ambitions—be they professional or amorous. ISBN 978-1-56478-726-2 / $16.00 US

Zaza Burchuladze
adibas / Translated by Guram Sanikidze
A "war novel" without a single battle scene, Zaza Burchuladze's English-language debut anatomizes the Western world's ongoing "feast in the time of plague." ISBN 978-1-56478-925-9 / $15.50 US

Tamaz Chiladze
The Brueghel Moon / Translated by Maya Kiasashvili
The novel of the famous Georgian writer, poet and playwright Tamaz Chiladze focuses on moral problems / issues, arisen as a result of the too great self-assuredness of psychologists. ISBN 978-1-62897-093-7 / $14.95 US

Mikheil Javakhishvili
Kvachi / Translated by Donald Rayfield
This is, in brief, the story of a swindler, a Georgian Felix Krull, or perhaps a cynical Don Quixote, named Kvachi Kvachantiradze: womanizer, cheat, perpetrator of insurance fraud, bank-robber, associate of Rasputin, filmmaker, revolutionary, and pimp. ISBN 978-1-56478-879-5 / $17.95 US

Zurab Karumidze
Dagny
Fact and fantasy collide in this visionary, literary "feast" starring historical Norwegian poet and dramatist Dagny Juel (1867-1901), a beautiful woman whose life found her falling victim to one deranged male fantasy after another. ISBN 978-1-56478-928-0 / $15.00 US

Anna Kordzaia-Samadashvili
Me, Margarita / Translated by Victoria Field & Natalia Bukia-Peters
Short stories about men and women, love and hate, sex and disappointment, cynicism and hope—perhaps unique in that none of the stories reveal the time or place in they occur: the world is too small now for it to matter. ISBN 978-1-56478-875-7 / $15.95 US

Aka Morchiladze
Journey to Karabakh / Translated by Elizabeth Heighway
One of the best-selling novels ever released in Georgia, and the basis for two feature films, this is a book about the tricky business of finding—and defining—liberty. ISBN 978-1-56478-928-0 / $15.00 US

www.dalkeyarchive.com